Virtue Discarded

Grace North

DDP
DEEP DESIRES PRESS
Winnipeg, Canada

Developmental editor: Margaret Larson
Proofreader: Francisco Feliciano

Published September 2023 by Deep Desires Press, an imprint of Story Perfect Inc.

Deep Desires Press
PO Box 51053 Tyndall Park
Winnipeg, Manitoba R2X 3B0
Canada

Visit http://www.deepdesirespress.com for more scorching hot erotica and erotic romance.

Virtue Discarded

Chapter 1

1880

Isabella Daniels would never forget the day that started her on her journey into a life of decadence. No one could have expected it, she was the curate's daughter. She dressed so cleanly and plainly, a smile from under her eyelashes for everyone, but she had a secret. The nice girl she pretended to be in public was not who she really was. The village near her father's church was quiet that day, the rain was keeping everyone inside. She made her way around the shops, pausing for a chat with anyone who would listen. Isabella was often left desperate for conversation, being stuck in the house all day with her parents. As an only child, her parents had kept a more than careful eye over her. She had to attend four sermons a week, read her Bible every night, and most of all, remember her virtue. Isabella would spend her whole time in church daydreaming. She thought about the young men in the village and which one she would like to kiss the most. Then her mind would go to where she wanted to live; she couldn't stay in her boring hometown forever. Her father had told her that women were naturally sinful, and because of that, they must work harder to keep a hold on the goodness that they were blessed with. To encourage her natural virtues, she was only allowed to wear the plainest of clothes, and stiff flannel beneath her unbleached corset. Isabella was often told off by the shopkeeper for standing around looking at the magazines and never buying. She poured over the fashion plates, showing what the society ladies in London were wearing, not that anyone ever dressed like that in her village. She had to remind herself of the towns and cities that existed outside of her tiny bubble.

With a sigh, she accepted that it was time to go home, knowing that her mother would ask her to brush out the fireplace. A flutter of paper caught her eye, wet pages dropped at the side of the road. Eager for a distraction, Isabella walked closer to investigate. "The Wild Irish Princess" the cover read.

"Probably some sort of cheap adventure story," Isabella muttered, flicking through the pages.

Her breath caught in her throat. Descriptions of kissing, wild and open-mouthed. Isabella's eyes widened. The things men and women could do together. She blushed, how had she not known about this?

Of course, she had heard snippets of conversation, from men standing outside the tavern.

She clutched the damp pages to her chest, knowing that this story needed further investigation.

Her heart thudded as she sat on her bed and spread the

pages around her. As her eyes moved down the page, her cheeks reddened. This was it; this was what she had been waiting for. The feeling spread to her stomach, in a tight knot, and then lower, she clenched her legs together. A handsome gallowglass had broken into a castle to rob it of its jewels, not expecting to run into the princess. Isabella was not too sure what a gallowglass was, but it didn't matter.

"I will not tell anyone that you have stolen my jewels," the princess whispered. *"If you give me something in return…"*

Over the following months, Isabella cultivated the dirtiest mind in her small village. She would use the money her father gave her for her allowance to buy dirty ballads and pamphlets from traders who passed through her tiny village. She loved to read about daring women with heaving bosoms, who could possess a man in ways that she could only dream of. She would read and treasure what she bought, hiding them away in a painted wooden box under her bed, and use what she had to fuel her fantasies.

And at twenty-two, all she had was fantasies, but this kept her going on her mornings scrubbing the kitchen floor. Or when she was sitting through one of her father's hour-long sermons, in her mind, she was dressed in silks, ready to have her way. Her mother wondered what had brought on these good moods, Isabella glared at her only half as much when she was given her list of chores for the day, and she had taken this as a sign that her daughter was maturing into adulthood.

Her mother sent her out to the shops on a rainy

morning, saying she would have a surprise for her when she returned to the house. Isabella pulled the hood of her cloak tight to her face against the wind and the rain. The road to the village was little more than a dirt track. Heavy carts had cut deep grooves into the road, which had filled with dark water, so she watched her step. She slung her empty wicker basket over her shoulder and sighed, wishing that her father would let her ride a horse. As if reading her thoughts, she heard the rapid thud of horses' feet. She stood up on the grass verge, holding onto a thorny branch from an overhanging tree, to avoid being splashed. The glossy chestnut horses pulled at the reins and snorted. They were hauling a huge carriage behind them. Through the glass in the side window, she saw a pale woman with dark red hair, who gave Isabella a sly smile, their eye contact did not break until the carriage was moving out of sight. On the back of it, she saw a huge gold and red crest. She stood for a minute, looking up the empty road, before climbing down again and continuing the walk, wishing that she could be a woman in a grand carriage, with no cares in the world.

She idly placed bruised vegetables into her basket, thinking about the woman that she had seen. As she was paying, she decided to get the local newspaper as well. She knew she would have to hide it when she got back to the house; her father did not like her knowledge of all the sin and the horror that existed in the world outside their home. The woman in the shop smiled warmly at her and thanked her.

Once outside, Isabella hid under the awning of the shop, and opened the paper, flicking to the advertisements.

She sighed with longing at the beautiful dresses, with their nipped-in waists, the bustles, and the flowing skirts.

Someday, it will be me wearing dresses like that, she thought. *And I won't be living here, it will be somewhere amazing.*

A small advert caught her eye; she recognised the crest as the one that she had seen on the carriage.

"Mordancross house, home of Lord and Lady Mordan seeks an energetic and loyal young woman as a maid. Uniform provided, as is bed and board. One day off per week and good pay. Applications in person only."

She thought of all the cleaning she did around the house, and how much she would like to be paid for polishing silver and making beds. The freedom of earning her own money as well, and not having to depend on the whim of her father.

My parents, she thought. *They would never let me leave. I'm going to be stuck at home with them, reading my Bible and drying up forever.*

She folded the newspaper and stuffed it into her basket. Hurrying back out into the wind and the rain.

The wind blew down her hood and cut through her clothes. Her hair went frizzy in the damp air, sticking to her face. She saw the smoke rising from the chimney of her house. She knew that a large fire must have been lit, which confused her, as they only ever did that for guests.

She pushed open the kitchen door, to find her mother waiting there.

"At last, Isabella! I thought you would never be back!"

she said, tsk-tsking at her soaked clothes. "I have filled a bath in your room, now go and be quick about it!"

When her mother looked away, Isabella grabbed the newspaper from the basket and darted up the creaky stairs. Steam rose from the tin bath in her bedroom, and her best dress was set out. Isabella squinted in confusion. She unbuttoned her damp dress and let it drop to the floor in an undignified heap. She admired her pert bottom in her hand mirror, almost grateful for all the walking that she did, and she knew that it would look even better in a pair of those black lacy knickers that she wanted so badly. She loosened the laces of her corset, wriggling slightly so that she breathed fully again. She pushed the clasps together, and let the heavy garment fall to the floor. The air in her bedroom felt cold on her naked skin; she'd set her knickers and vest on the bed, as she would wear them again.

Isabella dipped one toe in the water, surprised at how warm the bath was. She got in, letting herself slide downward, immersing herself. She was used to short and cold baths, in water that her parents had already used. She leaned her head back, feeling the tendrils of her dark hair escape from its bun. She let her back arch, raising her breasts to the cold air, letting her nipples harden. Droplets of water ran down her neck and between her breasts. She let her index finger trace downward, from below her chin, down the hollows of her neck, the sharpness of her collarbones, the roundness of her breasts, and then to the soft hair between her legs. She could pretend that her hand was someone else's, someone who wanted to appreciate every inch of her and make her feel amazing.

Every time she walked into the town, she had someone that she kept an eye out for. She had no idea what his name was, and she couldn't imagine what it would be. She knew that he worked at the stables; she saw him brushing down the impatient horses, or cleaning off the tack. She would sneak glances at him, hoping that he wouldn't notice. He wore tight trousers and high boots. His loose shirt showed his collar bones and a hint of chest hair. His dark, curling hair was tied back in a ponytail. Often, he kept a riding whip tucked into his belt or boot.

Isabella imagined pulling him up to the hayloft, not telling him her name. She would strip him bare first, scattering his clothes, but telling him to put those long boots back on, and she would push the whip in her head, his body lean and toned, his thigh muscles hard. But she could not picture what was meant to be between his legs. She had read many descriptions of what it should be like, but she could not imagine it yet. The man would reach for her, longing for her, but he wouldn't get her in the way that he was picturing. They would lie down together, a blanket covering the worn wood of the floor. Isabella would use a broken bridle to bind his hands, then, as he looked up at her, she would take her clothes off, and he could watch shadows dance across her body in the flickering candlelight. She would pull the whip from his boot and use it to tilt his face up toward her. She would straddle him as he lay there, his bound hands above his head. She didn't know what a cock was meant to look like, but she had read about what it would feel like. She would feel him push up into her, hard and deep, too enjoyable to be painful, pushing hot breaths out of her. She would look at his lovely face, long hair coming loose, strands of hay in it.

Isabella found her breaths getting shorter as she caressed her clit, but before she could finish herself, her mother called for her.

"Get dressed, Isabella! Try to look your best!"

The water in the bath was cooling, and she rolled her eyes as she clambered out. She put on her best dress. It was plain black, with touches of faded lace at the collar and cuffs. She combed the tangles out of her hair, then pinned it back up in a bun, leaving the back of her neck exposed.

Isabella was used to only having to wear her best dress to church, and then changing back into her everyday clothes as soon as she got home. She peeked over the banister, seeing light coming from under the door of the good room. She stepped down cautiously, disturbed by this sudden change in her routine. She could hear unfamiliar voices as she opened the door.

Two men and a woman sat on one sofa, and Isabella's parents on the other. They all sipped tea from the best china cups and saucers, and a large fire burned in the grate. They stopped speaking as she walked in, and her father gestured for her to sit between him and her mother. She sat and studied the faces of the three who sat opposite her. The older man smiled at her approvingly, showing long tombstone teeth. The pale younger man avoided her glance.

"This is our lovely daughter, Isabella," her father said with a grin.

Isabella was taken aback, unused to her father saying anything nice about her.

"She does look as lovely as you said," the unfamiliar woman said. "Strong, but still womanly. Is she good at cooking?"

"Oh, yes," Isabella's mother said. "She does most of the food preparation."

Isabella glanced between the two groups, confused and frustrated that they were talking about her without including her.

"Is she your only child?" the man asked.

Isabella's mother flushed, "I had three other children, but they died young."

The man and the woman murmured to each other, and the young man finally looked up at her.

"Yes, I think we like her," the man said.

"What is this about?" Isabella asked, breaking her silence.

"Your engagement," her mother smiled. "We weren't going to let you stay at home forever."

"Our son, Phillip, is going to be your husband. He can provide well for you; he's going to inherit my solicitors' office."

"Husband?"

Isabella stared at the pale and shy young man. His mousy hair curled over his ears and forehead. His clothes were fashionable but looked wrong on him. His wrists were skinny. He was not the kind of man that would stir any fantasies in Isabella. She swallowed, feeling a painful lump in her throat.

"The ceremony won't be huge, just a family event,

perhaps some close friends," her father said. "Perhaps in the next few months."

Her mouth was dry. A life with that man? She could feel herself beginning to shiver, but had to hold it in. She tried to steady herself by gripping the side of the sofa, unable to look at any of them. She had to stop listening to their conversation, she didn't want to hear anything more. All she knew was that she would have to run.

Chapter 2

After those strange new people had left, Isabella's parents went to bed. She sat up, legs crossed, on her bed. She looked around her small bedroom in the flickering orange candlelight. She knew it had to be the last night she spent in that room, or else she would be trapped with a boring young man for the rest of her life.

She had barely slept. Instead, she tossed and turned in a cold sweat. Every time she closed her eyes, she felt that young man's pale blue eyes staring at her. When the grey light of the morning broke through her curtains, she rolled out of bed and quietly started to pack her few belongings into a bag. She listened out for her father leaving the house, slamming the door as he headed out to give a sermon. Her mother was having some of her friends over, so she would slip out as they spoke in the kitchen. Isabella folded her clothes into the bag, placing the newspaper at the top, left open at the page with the job advertisement. She left the bag in the hall as she crept into her parents' room and pulled open the bottom drawer of the dresser, uncovering a small tin. She opened it and took a couple of notes and coins and shoved them into her boot.

She edged her way down the stairs, hearing her mother and her friends talking in excited tones in the kitchen. Isabella realised with disgust that they were probably discussing her engagement.

Overwhelmed with sudden feelings of sadness and freedom, she clicked the front door of the house closed behind her. She glanced back, almost expecting someone to run out and stop her, to drag her back, but nothing happened. Running would make her look too suspicious, but she made sure that her dark bonnet shielded her face, and she pulled her cloak tight around her. The road to the village felt longer than ever. A drizzle of rain started, and she could strongly smell the dust of the road. She passed the church, expecting her father to be waiting for her, but he was nowhere to be seen.

She kept her head down as she made her way through the village, passing people without glancing up. When she arrived at the stables, just behind the village pub, she saw the young man she had fantasised about, just before the revelation. He was somehow even more beautiful than he had been in her dreams. Maybe it was because she was in desperate need of his help. This was her chance to change the direction of her life, and she knew that she couldn't let it slip away.

"I'm looking to go somewhere," she said.

"Everyone is a little busy at the minute, would you be able to wait a while? It could be a few hours."

She narrowed her eyes and stepped toward him, looking up into his bright blue eyes.

Rain dripped down her face, and she fished the money out of her boot.

"I think I recognise you…" he started, looking intently at her.

"I'm in a bit of a hurry, I really can't wait around long." she told him, attempting not to blush under his gaze.

"I could say to someone…"

"Wait, listen to me, I really need your help," Isabella said.

He looked back at her; he seemed distracted.

She stepped towards him. "I don't have time to explain, I need to get away from here."

"I don't usually drive," he said. "'So you'll have to let me speak to someone, if you just give me ten minutes…"

Isabella didn't have time to wait; she had to convince him and fast. As he looked away to see if there was anyone nearby, she grabbed his necktie and pulled him down to her eye level. His eyes widened, and she could smell hay and sweet sweat. Then she kissed him, one hand on his face. His lips were soft, and he tilted his head in the opposite direction from hers, inviting her to kiss him more. His mouth opened under hers, and she could have cried for happiness. Her first kiss. She felt like one of the heroines in the stories that she loved to read.

"Where were you wanting to go?" he asked breathlessly.

"Mordancross House," she smiled.

"I could take you if you are all right with the open carriage."

She nodded and slung her bag over her shoulder. He harnessed up the horse, and she admired him. The day before, she would have only dreamt of something like that.

He took her hand and helped her up onto the front of the carriage with him. He whipped the horse into a trot, and she watched his face, noticing the tiny freckles across his pointed nose.

"I've seen you in the village before," he said after a quarter of an hour of silence between them.

"I've seen you too."

"You shocked me, you know?"

"I think that I shocked myself more."

"Why are you running?" he asked, not taking his eyes from the road.

"Who says I'm running?"

"I liked that kiss, a lot, and I could see it in your eyes that you wanted to, but I could feel your desperation."

"Well, you are good-looking," she sighed, blushing.

"And you are very pretty," he said, glancing sideways at her, "in a kind of up-tight way."

"I would be offended by that, but I know that I dress in a very dull way, but it's not my choice."

"So that's why you are running?"

They were in the countryside. The rain had let up, and the sun was making steam rise from the dirt road. The horse let out an unimpressed snort.

"No," she said. "I shouldn't tell you this, but I had to leave home to avoid being married off."

"Your secret is safe with me, don't worry about it.

Experience a bit of freedom before you have to commit to anyone."

"Getting that freedom seems like it's going to be difficult," she murmured. "I have so many things that I want to experience."

The carriage rolled through the countryside, Isabella thought about how close to home she had always stayed. Even the neighbouring villages were foreign to her, she had been living in a tiny world for so long.

Far ahead of them, Isabella could see the house. It was built from sand-colored bricks, with towering stacks of chimneys and too many windows to count. She clambered down from the carriage at the gates. She was stiff from sitting for nearly two hours.

"All the best," the young man said with a smile. "I hope that you find everything that you are looking for."

She handed him a couple of coins and waved to him as he left her. The cartwheels rumbled back along the road to the village. She turned toward the ornate, black iron gate. Ahead of her were narrow rows of manicured bushes, and ornamental ponds with scattered lily pads, and great orange fish beneath the surface. She lifted the heavy latch and pushed the gate open. The air was filled with the sweet smell of exotic flowers. Her stomach turned with nervousness as she walked up the path toward the huge house.

She rang the doorbell and stepped back, suddenly hoping that her hair had stayed in place and that she was not covered in dust from the road. The door was answered by a maid, who stood a head taller than Isabella. The maid said nothing, and Isabella found herself flushing.

"I'm here about the job advertisement."

There was a pause, as the tall woman looked down at her.

"Ah yes, the Mistress is in the library, if you will come with me?"

Isabella followed the maid through the bright vestibule and into the open hallway. The wood panelling shone, and her eyes were caught by the stained-glass window, halfway up the stairs, showing the family crest. She hurried after the other woman, who had opened a door into the vast library. The lady of the house was reclining on a red velvet sofa. Her deep red hair was loose and cascaded over her shoulders. When she looked over the top of the book she was reading, Isabella recognised her as the woman she had seen the day before in the carriage. The Mistress sat up.

"Please have a seat, Miss…"

"Isabella Daniels."

The Mistress waved away the maid who had stepped forward to pour the tea. Instead, the Mistress insisted on doing it herself. Isabella carefully sipped from one cup as the other woman watched her, examining her movements.

"You must be here about the advertisement for a new maid?"

"I am," Isabella replied, hoping she did not sound too eager.

"Interesting, and why do you want to work here?"

Isabella glanced around the room, at the ladders, the bookcases, and the stacks of leather-bound novels. "I have to let go of my old life, and I think that this is the perfect place to do it."

The red-haired woman raised an eyebrow. "Are you hardworking?"

"Yes."

"Are you a fast learner?"

"Yes."

"Then you are my new chambermaid. Follow Susa there, she will make sure you get everything that you need."

She sat and stared at her new Mistress for a few seconds, her legs refusing to let her get up. The woman smiled at her over her teacup. Isabella was stunned that she had got the job so easily. She followed the maid, Susa, up the main staircase, feeling the deep carpet beneath her feet. Susa was silent, walking with a sway, and Isabella noticed the start of a smug smile on her face. Susa opened a door into a small room. It was sparsely decorated, with only a long mirror and a clothes rack.

"I need you to strip off," Susa said. She had a tape measure in one hand, and she closed the door firmly behind them.

"What?"

"I need you to take your clothes off so that you can be measured for your uniform."

"But—"

"Don't worry, Isabella," Susa said, the corners of her mouth curling up. "It's not like I'm getting anything out of it."

Isabella flushed darker. She had just arrived, and already things were like a dream. She had never had anyone undo the stiff buttons of her clothing before. She felt Susa's deft fingers pushing the buttons through their holes. She gently pulled the dress from Isabella's shoulders and helped her to step out of it, leaving her standing in only her underwear, her loose chemise, and drawers. She shivered despite the heat of the room. The fabric was so thin that she was sure that Susa could see right through it, and Susa gripped her wrists before she could cross them over her chest.

"How am I supposed to measure you if you are trying to do that?"

Susa pulled the tape measure tight around Isabella's chest. Isabella could feel it against her nipples through the rough fabric of her corset. She felt Susa's breath on her face as her waist was measured.

When she was finished, she told Isabella that her first task would be helping the Mistress dress.

"What?" Isabella spluttered, "I don't know what I'm doing, and I don't have my uniform yet!"

"The Mistress prefers to teach people herself. She will not mind that you aren't practised. Meet her when she leaves the library, in her own time."

"But what if I make a fool of myself?"

Susa didn't answer. Instead, she grinned as if she liked the idea of that.

Chapter 3

Isabella stood at the bottom of the main grand staircase, fidgeting with nerves. She could not understand why she had been left alone in this big house already. She was looking up at the plaster ceiling, admiring the different carvings on it, when she heard a door behind her open.

"Hello, Isabella," the Mistress smiled. "So lovely to see you again. Will you come with me up to my dressing room?"

Isabella walked beside her up the main staircase, a little bit surprised that she was allowed to use this set of stairs. When Isabella was reading, even in dirty books, the lords and ladies in these big houses always seemed to have their servants scurrying around in a warren of hidden passageways and doorways. The Mistress looked over at her as if she were reading her mind.

"I let all my servants use the main staircase. All the people I have serving me are wonderful, so I am proud to have them seen around my house."

Isabella wondered if this was normal, she didn't think that it could be. From murmurs that she had heard around the town, employers in big houses did not treat their servants well, much as her parents had treated her. More and more she felt her old life drifting away, and she knew that her new uniform was going to be more glamorous than anything she had worn before.

"I will pay you better than anyone else would. All that I ask is your loyalty." The Mistress had an intense look in her eyes, as she glanced back over her shoulder.

"Of course."

"So, first, I am going to teach you about helping me dress. You will assist me with this when Susa is unavailable."

They went together into one of the rooms off the main corridor at the top of the stairs.

"This is my dressing room, and one of my bedrooms. I have a few other rooms, for other things."

She did not explain what, but Isabella knew she probably wouldn't understand anyway; rich people had more time and money than they knew what to do with.

Isabella's breath caught a little bit when she saw how beautiful the room was. The wallpaper was deep red, golden roses curling up it. The room was dominated by a four-poster bed made from dark wood. The Mistress opened a set of double doors to reveal all the clothes in the wardrobe.

"So, I want to dress for dinner, something elegant."

The Mistress ran her fingers over the dresses before drawing out a dark blue gown and handed it to Isabella.

"And for a dress like this one, I will need a matching corset and cover, dark gloves, my bustle cage…I know it's a lot to remember, isn't it? But you will learn, especially when you start to wear things like this yourself."

"I will get to dress like this?"

Isabella was eye level with the Mistress' mouth and could feel her gentle breaths in her hair as she unbuttoned the bodice. The metal buttons were warm from her body heat. The skirt was unlaced, and the Mistress stepped out of it. There was nothing vulnerable about her new Mistress, even dressed only in her petticoats and corset. It was Isabella who was feeling nervous and exposed. She was grateful when the Mistress turned her back to her, allowing her to loosen the tight corset strings. The Mistress glanced over her shoulder at her.

"Are you always this quiet?"

Isabella shook her head.

The Mistress laughed. "I suppose you are trying to make a good first impression on me. But you have nothing to fear, and I'm sure we will get to know each other."

Isabella was confused. Why was the Mistress putting so much effort into talking to her?

Isabella unclasped the corset and took it off. Under it, the Mistress was wearing a loose underdress, and Isabella swallowed, as she was able to make out her Mistress' sharp shoulders and the bones of her back. Under her petticoats, the Mistress was wearing short knickers that reached halfway down her thighs, and stockings with garters over the knee.

Isabella flushed darker as her Mistress turned back around. She could see through the thin fabric. She felt a stir deep in her stomach. This was another woman. Seeing her Mistress shouldn't make her feel like this.

"Help me dress now," the Mistress said with a

glittering smile, as her hands traced from her slim neck, down across her chest.

Before this day, Isabella had not thought about the intimacy of dressing someone. As Isabella closed the front clasps on the Mistress' corset, she was intoxicated with the smell of her exotic perfume. The Mistress turned around, and Isabella took the cords in her hands.

"Lace me very tight," the other woman murmured.

Isabella pulled, forcing a breath out of her Mistress.

"Sorry! Did I hurt you?"

"Don't apologise, you are doing what I asked you to do, now try again."

This time, Isabella pulled harder, and the Mistress let out a small moan, making Isabella cross her legs. She caught the other woman's eye in the mirror. Isabella hoped that she took her flushed face and red lips for exertion.

Isabella tied the laces in a bow and helped the Mistress step into the dress, which buttoned along the length of her spine. All the time, Isabella was being watched in the mirror.

Is this normal? Isabella wondered. *The way she speaks to me? The way that she looks at me? Is this happening in big houses all over England? Or is this something else?*

Isabella stepped out of the room, feeling slightly breathless. The other maid, Susa, seemed to appear out of nowhere, and Isabella knew that she must have been waiting for her.

"How did you find it?" she asked.

"Very good, good, yes," Isabella stuttered.

"I've done you the favor of bringing your belongings to your room, and I'll show you the way now."

"You'll be sharing with Catherine. Don't worry, she's a nice girl," Susa said, leaving her at the door.

Isabella knocked before stepping in. The room had a wardrobe, two single beds, and a door that led off into a tiled bathroom. A bath with lion's feet stood in the centre of it. Catherine sat on one bed. She had a notepad leaning on her lap, and she was gently tracing with a pencil.

"You must be the new girl," Catherine said. "I didn't think they would find anyone quite so quickly."

Catherine was about Isabella's age. Her light eyes were narrowed.

"I guess I must have stood out a bit," Isabella said, forcing a smile.

Catherine set her drawing to one side; she had been doodling what she could see out the window.

"I'll give you a quick tour of the house, so I can give you an idea of what you will be doing. The master and Mistress will be having many guests over for a party in a few days, so we will be busy."

Catherine led her down a long hallway. "This is all the servants' quarters. I'm sure you've seen that the rest of the house is much nicer."

"I've seen the front hall and the library."

"Well, we don't have to worry too much about where the kitchen is or anything. We work mostly in the bedrooms."

Isabella caught Catherine's gaze and the pair of them blushed.

"Not like that," Catherine stammered. "Don't know why you would be thinking about that."

Isabella giggled, breaking their tension, and making Catherine smile.

Isabella was shown the expansive drawing-room, the Turkish bath in the basement, and the bedrooms, each beautiful and made up in a different style and color.

"I think I'm going to be glad of the company." Catherine sighed once they had returned to their room. "It'll be good to be with a girl who is about my age."

"I'm glad you think so. I was worried that you might hate me."

"I am sorry that I gave off that impression. I was just being careful. Would running you a bath make up for it?"

When Isabella woke up, the water in the enamel bath was cold, and the gas light was still burning. She was confused about where she was and looked about herself, splashing water onto the tiled floor.

"You haven't drowned in there, have you?" Catherine called from the bedroom.

Isabella laughed and climbed out of the bath, pulling a warm towel from the rack, and tied it around her shivering body.

The bedroom was warm, and Catherine was lying back on her bed, sketchbook on her lap.

"I'm glad that you are still with us!" Catherine smiled. Her blonde hair had been loosened from its bun, and she had unbuttoned the top of her dress.

On Isabella's bed, a new uniform had been laid out. Beside it was a black corset, outlined with delicate pale lace, a few pairs of matching knickers beside it. She smiled as she lifted the corset, finding silky vests and corset covers. "Are these all for me?"

"Of course, they were left while you were passed out in the bath," said Catherine.

Isabella ran her hands over the expensive fabric. "It's all so lovely."

"The Mistress is very generous. If she likes you, she will give you more."

"Have you received much from her?"

Catherine flushed. "I've worked here for two years, but I rarely see her, never mind talk to her, so I haven't had the chance to make a good impression. But if you see her, you must remember to be polite, and only talk to her if she talks to you first."

Isabella glanced away, not wanting Catherine to know that she disagreed.

Her mood lightened as she tried on her new underwear, thrilled to finally get to wear silken stockings, instead of rough woollen ones. She got Catherine to lace her corset tighter than she was used to and put on her uniform. The lace at the cuffs and collar was soft and Isabella finally felt free, she had escaped her old life.

Chapter 4

Isabella woke early and lay in her warm bed, thinking of the lovely evening that she had had. She and Catherine had eaten their dinner outside, as they watched the deer in the park as they grazed and slept. She thought she saw her Mistress watching her. Isabella couldn't be sure in the light of the setting sun, but she would recognise that dark copper hair anywhere. She could conjure up her face in her mind easily: her eyes were a dark blue, and her skin was almost translucent. It was a warm evening, and Isabella slept easily between the cool and crisp sheets.

She dressed, admiring the pleated and flowing skirt, and the fitted bodice. Catherine was already up by the time Isabella arose and had got them their breakfast from the kitchen. Isabella ate a bowl of hot porridge with cinnamon, a ripe orange, and had a generous cup of milky tea.

Catherine took her along the plain servants' passage and opened a door out onto a corridor on the second floor of the house.

"Stripping the beds is going to be so quick, with there

being two of us! You take the left side of the hall, and I'll do the right."

Isabella opened the door to the first bedroom, gazing in to make sure that there was no one inside. It was the bedroom and dressing room that she had been in with the Mistress the previous night.

This is the kind of bedroom that I am going to have someday.

She touched the velvet curtains of the bed and sighed. She lifted a pillow to remove the cover, but out of the corner of her eye, she noticed a huge wardrobe, with figures of elegant women carved into it, she hadn't noticed the pictures the previous night. She could not resist opening up the doors to look inside. Vibrant dyes on silken fabrics. The scent of a sweet and flowery perfume rose from them. The waists of the bodices were small, and flared out in the chest, causing Isabella to think of the Mistress' figure. She had tried not to think about it too much before. The previous night, while Isabella was outside enjoying the dinner and the pleasant weather, she thought she saw her Mistress watching her. Isabella couldn't be sure in the light of the setting sun, but she would recognise that dark copper hair anywhere. She could conjure up her face in her mind easily, her eyes were a dark blue, and her skin was almost translucent.

She was shaken from her thoughts by the sound of the door handle slowly turning, and a laugh that did not sound like Catherine's. Isabella flung herself into the wardrobe without thinking, and pulled the heavy doors shut, leaving a crack to peek through. She held her breath.

The Mistress stepped into the room, laughing still, her head thrown back. She was followed by a well-dressed man, who Isabella did not recognise. He was tall, with dark hair that fell about his shoulders. He had a shadow of stubble on his chin, and he smiled as he loosened his red cravat. The Mistress pulled a clip from her hair, allowing it to cascade down around her neck, and down her back. Isabella watched from the dark wardrobe as their lips met. Isabella's stomach twisted in excitement, knowing that she was seeing something that wasn't meant for her. He unbuttoned the Mistress' dress, sliding his hands over her bare shoulders and pushing the dress down, allowing it to fall to the floor. He covered her neck and shoulders in kisses, their breaths growing heavy and ragged. Isabella could see the tip of his tongue on her neck, his full lips parted as he caressed her. Isabella was stunned, she remembered to breathe, letting it out in a gasp. She covered her mouth. She was on her knees, feeling herself getting wet. The Mistress was stripped of her dark knickers, to reveal her firm buttocks. She lay back on the bed and beckoned to the man. He gave a sly smile, pushing his hair off his face, and then he dropped to his knees obediently, and she put her legs over his shoulders, and she weaved her fingers into his hair and then pulled him toward her.

Isabella's breath caught in her throat as the man slid his fingers into his mouth, sucking them deep in, covering them in his saliva. She could hear the wetness of his mouth. His fingers lingered on his lower lip for a couple of seconds, Isabella's heart pounding in her ears. He then touched the Mistress between the legs, parting her lips with one hand,

and she gasped with delight. His fingers entered easily, and Isabella watched her flex with pleasure as he put his mouth to her clitoris. Isabella flushed, wishing she could get a hand between her legs, to touch herself, but she was terrified of them noticing her. She also longed for the man to remove his clothes, so that she could see what he looked like. The Mistress was pulling hard on his hair, her thighs tightening around him. Isabella watched from the dark wardrobe as he pushed his fingers into her, her back arching, and she listened to the sound of his lips on her. Her head was thrown back, a halo of red hair around her face, her face creased up.

"Thomas, there's something that I want you to do," she said, breathlessly.

"And what is that, my Mistress?" his face was damp from her.

Her long legs, dressed in knee-high sheer stockings and laced up boots, were still over the man's shoulders, the heels by his ears. "I want to hear you desperate for me," she whispered, a smug grin on her lips.

"Fuck me, Mistress," he said. "I want you to own me and do as you please."

"You will have to ask more kindly than that."

"Please, you know that I want this beyond anything else. I'll do anything."

"I think you have persuaded me!"

She easily got to her feet and pulled open the set of drawers next to the four-poster bed. She lifted out a dark wooden box and clicked it open to reveal an object wrapped in dark silk: an ivory phallus. The Mistress fixed a leather belt around her waist and fixed the dildo to it. She massaged an oil along the length, focusing on the tip.

"Bend over," she whispered, and he stood, feet apart, hands gripping the sheets that Isabella was supposed to have stripped.

The Mistress pushed his head down onto the mattress and stood behind him. Reaching around, she pulled his belt and revealed his buttocks. Isabella craned her neck, hoping to catch a glimpse of his cock.

With one hand on the dildo, she teased his opening. She poured the cool oil down between his buttocks, and he gasped.

"This is what you wanted," she whispered.

"This is what I want," he replied in a muffled voice, not raising his head from the bed.

He moaned gently as the Mistress began to press the fake cock into him, her hips against his buttocks as she guided it in.

"You're going to take it all, and you are going to love it," she hissed.

"Maybe just a little bit slower."

"You should know by now that the pace is set by me," she said, and he cried out as she pushed the dildo fully inside him.

Isabella watched as his muscles tensed in resistance, the Mistress raking her long nails across his shoulders and down his back. Whatever scratches she was leaving were hidden by his white shirt. Isabella felt her face burning. This wasn't just a dirty story; it was real life, and it was so much more than she thought it would be.

The Mistress suddenly stopped and glanced around.

"You are feeling it too then?" the man whispered.

"Yes," the Mistress said coolly. "We are being watched."

She slid the dildo out of him slowly, as he breathed heavily. Isabella drew back from the doors, wishing that she had somewhere better to hide. She glanced around, knowing that there was nowhere to go. The Mistress stepped back; the red flame of her pubic hair hidden by the dramatic curve of the dildo. Dark blue eyes raked the room.

"Try the wardrobe," the man murmured, pulling his trousers back up and buttoning them with one hand.

"I did like the feeling of you watching us," the Mistress sighed, as she flung open the wardrobe doors. "But I think you might enjoy yourself more if you came out and joined us."

Isabella cowered at the bottom of the wardrobe, uncomfortably sitting on several pairs of shoes. The Mistress offered her a hand, and Isabella took it, ashamed, her eyes caught by the dildo.

"I guess you had to meet the master of the house at some point," the Mistress laughed, not caring that she was wearing only her corset and a dildo.

Isabella saw her reddened chest and neck, hot from her exertion, her tiny waist, her strong thighs, but her attention went back to what was strapped between her legs.

"I suppose you have never seen one of these before," the Mistress smiled. "They are rather rare. I had to get this one specially made by a very subtle artist in Dublin."

"I've never…" Isabella stumbled over her words, as she tried to straighten her dress.

"Oh Thomas, I don't think the poor girl has ever seen a cock before. Have you, doll?"

Isabella shook her head, wanting to hide from her shame, her face burning under the gaze of two sets of eyes.

"I guess we can indulge you. A big treat for your first day. Thomas, stand over here, will you?"

Isabella was beckoned forward, and she took two nervous steps. Her corset suddenly felt too tight, and her legs shook. She could feel the Mistress's breath on the back of her neck. With one hand on her shoulders, the Mistress forced Isabella onto her knees. She only just managed to put her hands out to stop herself from falling too fast. The Mistress crouched down beside her, pushing Isabella's tied-up hair out of the way. Isabella jumped to feel soft lips on the back of her neck, the Mistress opening her mouth and nipping Isabella's soft skin with her teeth. Without thinking, she let out a deep moan, and the Mistress bit her hard.

"Let the girl see."

Isabella watched his slender fingers undoing the buttons on his trousers, her heart pounding. She saw the master's cock, hard and curving, deep blue veins stood out against his pale skin, leading up to the purple tip. Her breath caught in her throat as she looked at it. Isabella wanted desperately to know what it felt like. He ran his hand up the length of it, and she wondered what he was planning to do with it.

"Do you want to see what it does?" the Mistress whispered.

"Yes."

"Open that pretty mouth."

Isabella flushed, looking upward as he stepped toward her. He put one hand on her chin, and she parted her lips, knowing that her mouth was dry and nervous. He placed the head of his cock between her teeth and guided it slowly in. She tasted the wetness and the sweet salt, the cock huge and filling her mouth. Isabella shut her eyes, disbelieving, her knickers wet as she leaned forward, wanting to take the length in her mouth, longing to know how to please him. She felt it touch the back of her throat, and she gagged. He took it from her mouth, and it stood inches from her face, glistening with her spit.

"Oh girl, you are going to have to learn," the Mistress sighed from behind her. "Open wide and let him fuck your mouth, then I will show you how to please him."

Thomas tilted Isabella's chin upward, and she looked into his dark eyes, a grin forming on his lips. He ran his thumb along her lower lip, sliding his fingers into her waiting mouth, to open it as wide as was possible. He gripped the bun on the back of her head to hold her in place, and she felt herself throb with sexual frustration. He put the cock back into her mouth, rubbing it along the inside of her cheeks, and she felt her eyes water with the strain. Once again, the cock reached the back of her throat, but this time, she was ready, and she clenched her thumb in her fist, stopping herself from gagging. She let out choking breaths as he rammed into her mouth repeatedly, the Mistress watched approvingly.

"Now that you have got him prepared for me, I will show you what is done now."

The cock was pulled from Isabella's mouth, and still wet with her spit, it was taken into the mouth of the Mistress, who was kneeling beside her. The master of the house held her dark red hair back, as she ran her mouth slowly up and down his length, drawing her cheeks in, and sighing with pleasure. She gripped the base of the cock in one hand. She drew her mouth away, a line of spit leading from her mouth.

"Now I want you to try it. Work hard and you may be rewarded." She winked.

The master turned to Isabella once more. She opened her mouth obediently and let him enter. She placed one hand on it carefully and moved herself back and forth, her body swaying.

"You do not have to be so reluctant." He laughed, gripping her hair with one hand, and her chin with the other, forcing the cock deeper into her.

Isabella shut her eyes and sucked, feeling his cock throb. Soon she felt his cum rush into her, filling her mouth. The Mistress kissed her neck, pushing the hair escaping from her bun out of the way.

The master took his cock from her mouth. "Well done."

The Mistress turned Isabella's head and smiled to see her cheeks puffed out, her mouth still full.

"Swallow it all, and appreciate it."

Isabella gulped, the warm salt disappearing down her throat.

"Did you enjoy that?" the Mistress asked, getting back onto her feet.

Isabella nodded vigorously, her knees weak.

The Mistress extended one elegant hand to Isabella, her eyes glinting.

Chapter 5

Isabella could not think straight. She tried continuing to work, dusting mirrors and changing beds, but she was too distracted. She kept thinking back to the morning like it was a dream that she could never allow to fade. She didn't have a sensible thought left in her head.

But what did it mean?

She wondered as she ate her lunch. Would it happen again, or had it been a one-off? The Mistress, to Isabella, was living the dream, a dominant woman, a mansion filled with beautiful things, and a gorgeous husband willing to do anything to please her. And Isabella had tasted his cock.

Isabella sat in the servants' dining room, crossing her legs under her heavy skirts, feeling as though everyone could hear her thoughts out loud, and they would know what she had done.

Then a thought hit her. What if she wasn't the only one who had experienced that? What if all the servants had?

She looked up from her food and scanned the faces of

the other maids. Many of them were pretty. She saw Susa, who had enjoyed stripping her so much.

She struggled through the rest of the day with much on her mind, and many questions she wanted to ask Catherine. She returned to their room, hoping to get answers, but the bedroom was empty. She sighed and lay down on the bed, wishing that she could have the truth. Had she experienced something special, or was she another in a long list of servants that the rich couple had decided to mess with?

She thought that pleasing herself might clear her mind and put her to sleep, but as she hitched her skirts up, she noticed an envelope on the bedside table. She ripped it open and read it.

Meet me in the centre of the maze.

The writing was curved and bold, written in violet ink. She knew it had to belong to the Mistress.

Isabella stood in front of the mirror, the evening light drawing out the amber in her dark eyes. She unpinned her hair, letting it fall around her shoulders, and started to brush it through, leaving it smooth and shining.

"She has asked for me, personally," she whispered to herself, as she plaited her hair and wound it back up. "What kind of strange, made-up world am I living in? The Mistress of the house wants to meet me in the centre of the maze…"

Isabella didn't know whether to assume the best or the worst. She caught her own eye in the mirror.

"Who cares if the master and Mistress aren't everything they're cracked up to be. Let's have some fun," she told herself.

She remembered seeing the maze outside the house,

and as she made her way out to it in the dying evening light, she was glad she had found an oil lamp to borrow. Her heels sank in the grass as she walked into the dark hedges. In the maze, most of the remaining light was blocked by the leaves. She took a turn into a dead end and almost walked straight into the hedge. She walked with the lamp held out in front of her, tiring her arm. She could not tell how long it had been, but she finally found the centre of the maze.

Before her, was a glass-domed palm house, the wrought iron painted white, so it appeared to glow. She could see a warm light inside. As she turned the door handle, she could hear the Mistress' polished voice.

"Oh Isabella, you found me! Well done!"

The Mistress was lying out on a red sofa, her feet bare. She was wearing a dark green dress, cut low across her breasts, the sleeves were netted with a shimmering dark lace.

Isabella stepped toward her, almost tripping over a blanket that was laid out on the ground.

"Now, isn't this always how you imagined your first time to be?"

Isabella glanced around at the exotic flowers and felt the humid air on her skin.

"I don't know how I expected it to be, but this is closer to something that I would dream of."

"Sweet girl." The Mistress smiled. "I found myself wondering all day about you."

"You did?"

"Yes, I remembered seeing that lovely face in the rain,

but I also wondered how you look under all those clothes. If you would be so kind as to show me?"

Isabella stepped back and nodded.

"I hope that you are wearing my gifts to you."

"I am, Mistress." The last word came out sounding more nervous than she wanted.

Her hands trembled as she unbuttoned her dress. She avoided the Mistress' mischievous glance.

"You can turn away if it makes it easier," the Mistress whispered.

Isabella faced away from her as she let her dress swish onto the damp ground. She felt the hot damp air on her bare skin, a droplet of water trickled down between her breasts.

"Face me."

She turned back, her dress at her feet. The Mistress nodded with approval.

"I think you will do perfectly." The Mistress grinned, perfect, white teeth showing.

"You have this false modesty, but that is not really you, is it? You pervert."

Isabella flinched.

"Don't look so upset." The Mistress laughed, sitting up. "I didn't mean it as an insult. I want to enjoy your body, and I am not interested in taking things further unless you think you will enjoy it as well."

"This morning," Isabella murmured, shifting her hands, unclasping her corset, unsure of whether she wanted to conceal her body or not. She dropped the corset to the floor. "It was pretty amazing...I didn't think that I would ever see anything like that."

"And you didn't just get to watch, you got to experience it as well."

Isabella pulled her shift off over her head, leaving herself wearing her knickers and stockings.

"Not everything was perfect though," the Mistress tutted, wagging a finger. "You certainly didn't finish tidying that bedroom, and that is the kind of careless mistake that I want to stop you from making."

"I'm sorry, I'll not do it again," Isabella said. She didn't think that the Mistress cared.

She was conscious of the Mistress' dark eyes taking in all the aspects of her body, her toned calves, her gaze lingering on a drop of water running down to Isabella's hip bone.

I'm just like a girl in a story, Isabella thought. *If I pinch myself, I might wake up, but, dear God, don't let me wake up.*

"Come over here for me."

Isabella walked forward, unsure of what she was expected to do. The Mistress pulled her over her lap, making her gasp. She laughed as she caressed up the back of Isabella's legs, feeling the seam of the stocking and making her shiver. She reached the top, and her sharp nail touched the skin of her thigh.

"Are you scared, Miss Isabella?"

Isabella had buried her face in the Mistress' skirts, attempting to conceal her increasingly heavy breaths, the smell of expensive perfume burning in her nose.

"I'm not afraid," she whispered.

"Good."

The Mistress pulled Isabella's knickers down, leaving

them around her ankles. Isabella tried to glance back, but her head was pushed down. Her dark hair was sticking to her face and neck in the humid air. A finger traced over her buttocks, and the Mistress cupped her cheeks.

"Shivering, when it is so warm in here?"

Isabella's legs were gently eased apart, and one hand crept between her thighs and found her opening. The Mistress smiled as she felt the wetness on her index finger.

"So tight," she murmured in satisfaction, gliding her middle finger slowly in.

Isabella tensed up, her back rigid.

"I need you to relax," the Mistress whispered. "I want you to like me getting a feel for you."

Isabella felt the finger move in, up to the knuckle, and she gasped, feeling the index finger finding its way in as well. "How does it feel?"

"I feel so…full," Isabella moaned.

"Oh? How do you ever expect to get a good fucking with that kind of attitude?"

Two fingers of the Mistress' right hand were deep in Isabella, and she raised her left hand, bringing it down hard on her ass, making her cry out.

"You did not do a very good job of cleaning that bedroom, so a little punishment is in order, and you are going to thank me for this."

Isabella could still feel the sting as the Mistress drew her fingers out of her. Another slap shook her, and the fingers were driven back into her, forcing a breath out. The Mistress fingered Isabella, sliding in and out faster and harder, all while spanking her hard across the ass. Isabella no longer knew if she was crying out from the pain or the violent pleasure that she was feeling. With each thrust of the Mistress' hand between Isabella's legs, she became wetter, and she throbbed hard in longing. She buried her face, tears forming in her eyes, her mouth opened as she gasped for breath. The Mistress stopped abruptly, and Isabella lay in her lap, trying to get her breath back.

"Sit up."

She sank onto the sofa next to the Mistress, who was offering her a glass of water.

"Since you did some things well, I am going to reward you. Get down on your knees."

"A reward?" Isabella asked, getting onto the blanket that had been laid out on the ground.

"A lesson for you."

The Mistress pulled her skirts up, revealing her long legs, concealed in dark stockings with lace tops. She was not wearing any knickers. She leaned back into the cushions, and Isabella leaned in toward her. The dark red hair formed into a perfect "V", and her clit stood out, pink and ready. Isabella pulled it into her mouth with her tongue and gently began to suck. The Mistress placed one hand on the back of Isabella's head, as she began to rock her hips against her face. Isabella could taste her sweetness on her lips, and without thinking, she used her index and middle fingers to part her lower lips, and push them deep inside, feeling the hot, wet, arousal. The Mistress let out a shuddering moan and pressed herself hard against Isabella's face.

"I love a fast learner," she breathed. "You must have learnt about this somewhere before!"

Isabella had. A few months before, she had bought a pamphlet off someone travelling through her village. The ink was cheap and smudged, and the story was like nothing that she had read before. It was about a tropical island, inhabited only by women, and these women had enjoyed ravaging each other, especially with their mouths. Isabella had poured over the descriptions of how to please a woman, confused and excited by it.

As the Mistress ground into her face, Isabella used three of her fingers to get as hard and deep into her Mistress as she could. She felt the muscles tighten and flex around her fingers as she pumped them in and out, each penetration making her Mistress cry out. The Mistress' hand was tight on Isabella's hair, and as she climaxed, she pulled her legs tightly around Isabella, leaving her almost unable to breathe. As the Mistress loosened her grip, Isabella sucked on her wet fingers, and seeing the Mistress' cunt before her, she could not resist venturing her fingers back into her. But as she tried, the Mistress pulled hard on her hair, and she looked into the dark blue eyes of the wealthy woman.

"You do what I ask, not what you want to do," the Mistress hissed. "It would be better for you if you remembered that."

The back of Isabella's head hurt from the strain, she nodded slowly.

"You should get up now." The Mistress sighed. "I'm sure that you will have many things to do tomorrow."

Isabella got to her feet, and the Mistress was smiling to herself and looking relaxed.

"I will send you a present," she said. "I want you to know that you are appreciated."

Isabella beamed, the pain at the roots of her hair easily forgotten. She reached down to pick up her clothes, but the Mistress grabbed her wrist.

"No, I want you to walk back up to your room completely nude."

"Really?" Isabella said, stunned. "But what if someone sees me?"

"Your body is enchanting. You have nothing to be ashamed of, so remove everything, and then you can leave."

She rolled her stockings, not believing what she was going to do. She tossed the last of her clothes onto the tiled floor, not trying to hide her frustration. The Mistress raised an eyebrow at her.

"Do what I want, and you will find your time here incredible," the Mistress called, as Isabella walked out the door of the palm house.

A gentle breeze had picked up, and she sighed as she tugged the door closed behind her. The grass path in the maze was cool under her feet, and she crossed her arms tightly across her chest. The leaves of the bushes rustled, and she could imagine hundreds of eyes hidden in the hedges, pushing back the branches, so that they could watch her, naked and vulnerable.

She picked up her pace, knowing that the quicker she was in her room, the less chance there would be of someone seeing something that they shouldn't.

She reached the end of the maze. The darkened house sat at the far end of the open lawn. She shuddered. Then, cupping a breast in each hand, she ran. She could not stop to think of the slugs and the frogs living in the wet grass. All she wanted was to be warm and clothed.

Breathless, Isabella arrived at the back door. She peered through the glass. Once she was sure that the door was open, she slipped into the house. Most of the building was in darkness, but light was escaping from under the scullery door.

Some of the servants must still be awake, she thought. *So, the back corridors might be risky.*

The front hallway was blackened and silent, and the heavy curtains were drawn shut. On all fours, Isabella crept up the curving staircase. The sixth stair let out a deep groan. Her eyes widened and she froze, certain that someone must have heard her. A door closed.

"Elizabeth, my love, is that you?" the master called.

Without further thought, Isabella darted up the rest of the stairs. By the time she slammed her bedroom door, she was panting, and a sheen of sweat had formed on her skin. Catherine sat up with a start, clutching her duvet to her chest. Isabella attempted to cover herself with the blanket from her bed.

"What on earth are you doing?" Catherine hissed, her eyes bright circles in the dim light of the room. "Are you naked, wandering about the house?"

Isabella pulled her nightdress on. "I was with the Mistress."

"Doing what?"

Isabella paused, knowing that no matter what she said,

it would sound awful. "The Mistress has chosen me. She wants me, and I help fulfil her desires."

Tension hung between the two girls. Catherine took in a sharp breath. "So, she is…making love to you? Another woman?"

"Yes," Isabella sat down on the bed.

"So, is that why she hired you? You lied to me! You aren't a maid at all!"

"Keep your voice down," Isabella whispered. "I didn't lie. I came here to work, cleaning and whatever, but then this happened."

"Aren't you just a normal girl? Why are you doing this?"

"She buys me things," Isabella said. She could see another parcel on her bed.

"But do you enjoy it?"

Isabella's mouth was dry. She didn't know how to reply.

"You should only be doing it if you enjoy it. Have you always thought about women in that way?"

"No." Isabella scowled. "Well, actually, I don't know, I've never thought about it too much." She had read many stories about women who fucked other women, but it had never struck her as being wrong, only different.

"I don't have a problem with it if you do enjoy it," Catherine whispered. "You are allowed to have fun, and there are far worse things that you could be doing."

"You think so?" Isabella asked, but she was considering what Catherine would think if she had known about Isabella's run from home.

"The main thing that you should be afraid of is her

getting bored of you. What will happen if she doesn't like you anymore?"

"Well, I will just have to stop that from happening."

Chapter 6

"This is for you," Catherine said, shaking Isabella awake.

She pointed to a blue, satin walking dress that hung on the back of the door. She then handed her a thick letter.

Catherine watched as Isabella ripped it open. A letter and a card fell out. The card read "Isabella Daniels, you are invited to my masquerade ball."

"There's going to be a dance tomorrow night." Isabella smiled.

"I know." Catherine sighed. "That's why we have to be preparing the spare bedrooms, there are going to be so many guests."

"Like me."

"What do you mean?"

"The Mistress has invited me."

"So, you get to have an amazing night, and I still have to work?"

Isabella let out a quiet giggle as Catherine slammed the door behind her.

The letter read:

So, Isabella, are you excited to be attending the ball? You should be.

Don't worry, I will not tell anyone that you are my maid. I'll make everyone think that you are the orphaned daughter of some esteemed magistrate, no one will question me.

I will provide a dress for you; I couldn't allow you to pick one yourself because I am unsure whether I can trust your taste. All you need to bring is yourself. Stay wonderful for me, Elizabeth.

Isabella lay back on the bed, smiling to herself, knowing that the new corset she got the previous night would look amazing with whatever dress the Mistress had chosen for her.

"I'm not leaving you alone this time." Catherine sighed as they dusted off mirrors.

"Maybe the Mistress wants you to leave me alone." Isabella grinned. "Maybe she is just waiting for you to go so she can come in here and ravage me."

Catherine flushed and looked toward the ground. "You shouldn't talk like that. You need to be careful, for your reputation…"

"My reputation? Do you mean if people knew about what I have done? Masters and Mistresses must have their way with servants all the time, and it never ruined what people think of them."

"Isabella, you should know that the wealthy can do a lot of things that people like us never could."

"You are making it sound as if she is forcing me to do this, but it's not like that at all."

"But do you tell her what you want?"

"Well, no."

"So, she is controlling you. She could tell you to do anything."

"I would love to be the one in control, but she would never let me."

After lunch, Isabella decided to take a walk to the stables. The horses were housed in a sturdy red-brick block, a clock tower pointing upward, a weathervane creaking in the wind.

A bay horse whickered as she stroked his velvet nose.

"What's your name, handsome?" she asked, scratching behind his long ears.

"His name is Bracken," a male voice said from behind her. "Unless you were asking me, in which case, my name is Garrett."

She turned to face him, and her mouth dropped open as she recognised the young man who had taken her to the house, her first kiss.

"I know who you are now, Isabella. But even without your name, I was unlikely to forget you."

"You again?"

"You're the pastor's daughter. Your parents have been looking for you."

She felt a pang of guilt, which was quickly replaced by the fear of them knowing where she was.

"They think that you are dead, or worse."

"Worse?" she asked.

"In church, your father has been warning everyone about wayward and perverted women." Garrett rolled his eyes, the corner of his mouth turning up.

"You aren't going to tell him where I am, are you?" she said, backing away from him. She did not want to have to run again, not after finding a lifestyle that she could make work for herself.

"I wouldn't do that. What you do is up to you. Besides, I work here now as well, and it's good to see a familiar face."

"So, you are here to look after the horses?"

"Yes, I understand wanting to get out of that village, it felt so small and closed in."

"You better not have followed me here because of that kiss. I don't know what I was thinking."

"Oh, don't worry, I didn't think anything of it." There was a glint in his eyes.

Isabella turned and walked out. The courtyard was filled with noise. Men were shifting tables and barrels of wine into the house. She nodded to a man at the door, and he dipped his hat in response.

She found her bedroom empty, and she sighed with relief. Garrett knew her story and her family. If he decided to, he could ruin everything, and she would be hauled off home and made the property of one of the dullest and most unattractive young men she had ever met. Garrett had power over her, and she rolled her eyes at the notion. Grimacing, she realised that she would have to stay on the right side of him.

Maybe saying that that kiss was unimportant was a bad

idea, she thought. *But I can't take it back now. I'll just have to try to be more careful in the future.*

She thought about that first kiss again, her conflicting feelings of fear, excitement, and arousal. She almost drooled.

I can't think of him in that way! she scolded herself. *If the Mistress caught me, God knows what she would do!*

She sat down. *Come to think of it, I'm not too sure how this relationship between the Mistress and I is supposed to work? We can't be exclusive, because she has her husband, so could I possibly have someone else too? But I know that it is one set of rules for her and completely different ones for me.*

She had so many questions, about her Mistress, and Garrett. He had looked more attractive to her than ever, with the sun behind him, a smug smile on his face as he confronted her.

Did he come here because of me? she wondered. *Or am I getting a bit full of myself?*

Her thoughts were interrupted by a loud knock at the door. The tall and elegant Susa stood in the doorway when Isabella answered the door. "I am here to help you to get ready."

"Really? Well, I don't need your help. I can sort myself out."

"Isabella, this masquerade ball is extremely important. The Mistress is insisting that you look as lovely as possible."

Susa stepped into the room, closing the door behind her and turning the key in the lock. The wooden chair from the bathroom was placed in the middle of the bedroom floor, and Susa sat down, crossing one leg over the other in her tight skirts.

"Get undressed, then I can help you with getting ready."

Isabella glared at her. "I didn't feel like I could stand up to you the last time, but I don't see why you need to watch me."

"Isabella, don't be so prudish with me. The Mistress has told me about what you get up to."

Despite feeling stronger than the last time she had encountered Susa, she felt a flare of embarrassment. She should have known the Mistress would not have kept it a secret.

"Well, Susa, if you want to see, I won't deprive you of it."

She tossed her head and stripped, drawing up more confidence than she knew she had.

All the time, she did not break eye contact with Susa, who was starting to blush.

"Not used to girls acting like this, are you?" Isabella asked, letting her corset drop onto the floor.

Susa's mouth was open as Isabella caressed her nipples with cool fingers, bringing them to hardness.

"You wanted me to act all ashamed and cower, didn't you? But I'm kind of enjoying this now. So, are you going to help me get ready or not?"

Susa curled Isabella's hair, laced her up, and dressed her in a dark velvet dress, cut daringly low across the bust, and her pale shoulders glowed through expensive floral lace.

Isabella brushed a tendril of hair off her face and smiled

as she admired herself in the mirror. She had never felt so beautiful.

The ballroom was already hot and crowded when she arrived. She hovered at the side of the room, sipping at champagne and nibbling on the elaborate food. She was hoping to catch a glimpse of a familiar face. The confidence she had had while dressing was easily lost. Every sliver of conservation she heard was something she didn't understand, something about grain prices, or ancient Greek literature. Isabella looked around desperately, not wanting to be left standing alone.

Over the sound of the chatter and the orchestra, she couldn't hear what was being said, but across the room, she could see the Mistress talking with a dark-haired girl serving drinks. The Mistress touched her hand, and the girl giggled. Isabella felt her stomach sink, and she had to look away so that she could control her temper. She took a deep breath and stormed across the room, hitching up her dress with one hand. She grabbed the Mistress' hand, enjoying the shocked expression on the serving girl's face.

"Dance with me, Elizabeth," Isabella murmured.

She could feel many eyes on them, taking in the rare sight of two women dancing together. Isabella led her Mistress in a fast and close waltz, their chests pressed together as they stepped and turned.

"I had not imagined that a maid would be able to dance so well." As she spoke,

Isabella could smell the sweet wine on her hot breath.

"My mother thought that it would be a useful and

ladylike skill to have. Though you may notice that I am using these skills in a way that would outrage her."

"You confuse me, Isabella. I hadn't expected this from you."

The master was watching them intently, hands clasped together.

"I think that someone else would like a turn," the Mistress laughed, and Isabella stepped back, expecting that the couple would want to dance together. The master put a hand on Isabella's waist, and she stared upward at him, as he smiled tightly back.

Her dance with the Mistress had left her breathless and excited, but the master was a change of pace. He was not listening to the tempo of the song. Instead, he swayed with her slowly and refused to look away from her. Somehow this made her feel more awkward than a more ferocious dance would have. She was finding it tough to believe that this was the same man that she had given a blowjob to.

"It has been lovely weather, hasn't it?" he asked, breaking her concentration. His dark eyes looked almost black in the evening light. The last time she had seen him, she had barely taken in his appearance. Now, in the ballroom, she was able to look at him, uninterrupted. His eyelashes were long and dark, and his skin was almost as pale as the Mistress'.

"I've been sleeping with the window open; it's been so warm."

He smiled, despite how handsome he was, she did not feel intimidated by him. There was a hint of red on his cheekbones. "You should have a walk around the deer park if you haven't already. Don't worry, the deer will keep well away from you."

"I will." She felt shy, realising that this must be how courting couples would speak to each other.

"We should step outside; this room is terribly hot."

She nodded and followed him across the crowded dance floor, avoiding couples absorbed in each other's company, and well-dressed women, drunk on too many glasses of expensive wine. They stepped out the patio doors into the paved rose garden. The sky was dark and clear, a sliver of white moon shone above the trees beyond the maze. The air was heavy with the scent of flowers and alcohol. Couples sat close to each other on the benches. "This is a wonderful night," the master murmured.

"I'm so glad that I could be here, I've never been to anything like this before."

"What a waste," the master tutted, using one gentle hand to tilt her head to face him. His wedding ring brushed past her chin. "How could a girl like you have grown up, never being allowed out?"

"I guess I didn't cope too well with it, but I survived by reading a lot, and having huge dreams." She was trying not to seem nervous around him.

"And have you found what you were looking for?"

"I think that I am closer than I have ever been."

"Let's do something terrible, Isabella," he looked conspiratorial, glancing around.

"Terrible? What do you mean?"

"Another experience for you, but this time, it would be just the two of us."

"But isn't that risky? We would get into all kinds of trouble if the Mistress discovered us!"

"The Mistress? You are such a sweet servant. I know that you are tempted, aren't you?" He leaned in close to her, and she could see the bright excitement in his eyes, glinting like amber. Her heart pounded, as she knew that he wanted her. "You are inexperienced, but you don't want to stay that way. This could be how you own a man's soul, Isabella."

"Could I own you?"

"We will have to see about that."

They crept around the side of the house, lights blazed from most of the windows, only the lower floor, where the kitchens were, was dark. They went inside through the same door that she had used after her adventure in the maze. Once the lights were on, the kitchen felt warm and safe. Pots and bags of flour lay abandoned on tables and counters, as the kitchen maids and cooks had left it.

"I know we both want this, but is it a good idea?" Isabella asked, her back against one of the counters, cool and hard. "The Mistress will be looking for us, she will have to notice that we are gone."

"Elizabeth will be far too distracted with some attractive stranger to notice that we are missing. Now turn around."

She shivered as he unbuttoned her dress. His lips touched between her shoulder blades, and she longed for him to tear the expensive dress from her body, and for him to fuck her hard. Instead, he took his time. He loosened the laces of her corset, set her dress over a stool. She wriggled out of her knickers and slipped her stockings down her legs.

He cupped his hands over her breasts, and he bent her over, placing her hands on the floury counter. His hands moved around from her hip bones to her ass cheeks. He held the cheeks apart as he pushed his cock into her. She gasped, no warning had been given. She arched her back and leaned her head back as he pushed his cock into her. He felt huge inside her, hard and pulsing. She hadn't even heard him take his trousers down. All the books she had read could not have prepared her for what he felt like.

He feels so big, and hard, she thought, picturing how his cock had looked. *I'm amazed it all fits inside of me.*

"I'm enjoying myself already," he sighed, taking a handful of her hair and pulling hard.

The first thrust had Isabella seeing stars. She tightened around him and pushed her body back into him, allowing the length to fill her. She could feel his hip bones against her buttocks. He took her by the hips and began to slide his cock in and out, each movement having her longing to spread herself wider. He felt no need to hold back his moans of pleasure.

"More," she whispered back to him. He felt amazing, better than she thought it would.

"Oh?" he said, breathlessly.

He stopped moving, and she glanced back at him lifting a container of olive oil, and carefully he massaged it onto two of his fingers.

"Look ahead and relax," he murmured.

His cock was still inside her as his index finger moved between her buttocks. He ran the oily finger down to her asshole, and he grinned as she gasped at the coolness of the oil. This was a part of her body that she had not experimented with, and she felt nervous as he toyed with the opening. She struggled not to tense up as he glided his index finger into her. His finger felt so large and deep in her, and he kept it in her as he began to thrust again.

"I don't always want to be the one who is being controlled and told what to do," he said, panting. "So, I'm glad that she found you. You are someone that I can take whatever I want from."

She narrowed her eyes at this. "But what if I would like to control you as well? What if I want to feel like her?"

He stopped fucking her and used her shoulder to turn her to face him, their hips together, his cock hard against her.

"A young and inexperienced chambermaid? To own me takes years of practice. It is not something that can be ordered and learned overnight. Elizabeth is so skilled; she is amazing in hundreds of different ways. Both of us had experienced many different people before we met, and she had had her share of thieves, judges, and farmhands. But when she tells me what to do, all of me wants to do it. I want her to command and punish me, and I think that I want to command and punish you. I want to see that flaring look in your eye as I scold you, how you pretend to resist."

Isabella felt her knees weaken at his words. He turned her away from him, and with one hand on the back of her neck, she was bent over again. Her drool dropped onto the floury counter.

"Keep your head down, and close your eyes."

She leaned against the counter in nervous anticipation

until she felt a strike across her ass cheeks as the master spanked her with a wooden spoon. She cried out, almost in relief.

"See, isn't this fun?" he asked. "You are helping me to feel so powerful and in control, and you like it, don't you?"

He slipped a finger into her, then drew it back and tasted it. "You do like it. Oh dear,

Isabella, you haven't been allowed to have a sweet release yet, have you?"

"And how would you know that?"

"Elizabeth has told me about everything that you have done together. She keeps a highly detailed diary of all her decadent adventures, sometimes she reads it to me, knowing how it frustrates me. I was sitting, alone, upstairs, while you were out with her, her fingers deep inside you."

She pulled away from him and sat up on the counter, with her long legs dangling. She pulled the wooden spoon out of his hand and gave him a satisfied grin. She tapped him on the shoulder with the spoon.

"Onto your knees, sir."

"You surprise me, Isabella."

She pulled him by the hair to between her legs, "I'm doing a lot of that tonight. You are going to make me cum, because I deserve this. I've been waiting for too long."

"It would be my pleasure. I don't want you to have to wait any longer."

The tip of his tongue was on her clit, so lightly that she could barely feel it. He gripped her hips, and took her clit between his lips, nipping it with his straight teeth. She put her legs over his strong shoulders.

"The whole time that I have been in this house I have been waiting for this!" she cried out. "I am getting what I've always wanted!"

His fingers were deep inside her, and he had taken her clit into his mouth. She let out ragged gasps for air, as her eyes rolled back into her head. "Yes...yes!"

Her mouth was dry, and her whole body trembled as she was finally able to orgasm. She slumped back onto the counter, her energy spent. As she lay there, he ran a cloth under a tap and wiped down her floury and exhausted body. She smiled to herself, pulling her legs up toward her chest. She let out small chirps of happiness as he cleaned between each of her toes. He kissed the soles of her feet. Once he was done, he helped her back into her clothes and combed out the tangles of her hair with his fingers.

"We both look a bit of a state," he smiled. "But I am hoping that everyone at the party is so drunk by this point that no one will notice."

"My dress is covered in flour, and all of my hair has come down!" she exclaimed, shaking her head.

He put one hand softly on her shoulder, and she looked up into his dark eyes. Their lips met, and he opened his mouth under hers, hot and desperate. His lips were softer than she felt any man's could be. His hands raked through her hair and down her back.

"We need to get back to the ball," he murmured. "The longer we are away, the larger the risk we are taking."

"You are right."

They dragged their heels as they trudged back up the stairs. In the dark hallways, Isabella longed to push her master up against a wall and have her fun all over again. At first, she had felt nothing but happiness, knowing that she had made her master submit to her and that he had brought her to orgasm. Despite all his protests, she had owned him, even if it was only for a little while. But once they had left the dim servants' corridors, a sick nervousness had crawled into her stomach. They strode into the ballroom, Isabella keeping her back straight, looking ahead as though she had nothing to hide. The Mistress stood at the opposite end of the room, arms folded, and Isabella knew that she had been sunk. The Mistress beckoned to her, and she had no choice but to go to her. She felt all the fancy food that she had eaten threaten to come back up.

"I have been looking for you, Isabella, where did you vanish off to?"

Chapter 7

The Mistress had her hand in a tight grip, and Isabella stumbled in her high shoes as she hurried along beside her. The Mistress had not spoken a word since they had left the ballroom. Isabella had frantically looked around, hoping to catch a glimpse of the master, wishing that he would take responsibility for what had happened between them.

The Mistress opened a door into a dark room and pushed her inside. She stood in the centre of the room, hopping from foot to foot. She eyed the shadowy shapes of the furniture. As the Mistress turned up the oil lamps, filling the room with a warm and flickering orange light, Isabella grimaced, unable to see the Mistress' expression. As the Mistress locked the door, Isabella took a better look around; she had not been in this room before. It was similar to many of the other bedrooms in the huge house, tastefully and expensively decorated. A dressing table and gleaming mirrors stood in one corner. The bed was the one piece of furniture that stood out. It was a carved wooden four-poster, but the beauty of the bed was not what made it unique. From each post came a leather strap with silver buckles. Isabella swallowed.

"I haven't seen this room before," she said with a laugh, attempting to break the tension.

The Mistress still had a face like thunder, her eyebrows drawn and her mouth turned down. "Get on the bed, on your hands and knees."

She felt clumsy in the long dress as she mounted the bed.

"You know that what you did was wrong, don't you?" The Mistress sighed as she strapped Isabella's wrists down.

"You didn't tell me what I could and could not do," Isabella protested, trying to meet her eyes.

"You are an adult," the Mistress said. She had shifted around, yanking Isabella's shoes off and fastening the buckles. "I should not have to tell you that it is wrong to play with things that are not yours. I thought that you could be trusted."

"I can be trusted! But he was very persuasive, and I had no idea that you would mind!"

"Isabella, you are a sweet girl, but sometimes you can be so stupid." The Mistress paced around, her heels loud on the wooden floor.

Isabella was on all fours on the soft bed sheets, the restraints tight around her ankles and wrists. The Mistress pulled Isabella's dress up, and then her knickers down to her knees.

"Look, I'm sorry, I don't really know what more you expect me to say."

"Don't worry, sweetheart, I'll know when you have begged me for forgiveness enough."

Isabella was breathing heavily, trying to figure out what the Mistress had planned for her.

"Your little cunt must be tired out after all of that fun you had earlier. Do you think it could take one more little thing?"

"If that would make you feel better."

"All right then, I know just the thing."

The Mistress rummaged through some drawers, making interesting noises as she consulted different boxes. Isabella knew that she was drawing it out to make her tenser. She finally chose a box and set it on the bed next to Isabella. The Mistress drew out a silk scarf and tied it over Isabella's eyes.

"I wouldn't want to spoil the surprise, and I always find that a blindfold makes everything feel endlessly more intense." She leaned in close to Isabella's ear. "And I know you want to feel all of this."

The Mistress used one hand to separate Isabella's legs. The box clicked open, and there was a rustle of cloth. The Mistress sighed with satisfaction. Isabella felt shivers creep up her spine, and she began to sweat with nervousness. The Mistress was already an intense person, so Isabella feared how she would act when angered. She heard a giggle, and turned her head, forgetting that she was unable to see. She felt something pushing into her, almost unable to fit into her opening.

"This is the biggest one in my collection, and it is a struggle even for me, so I'm interested to see how you cope."

Isabella tried to relax to allow it to enter more easily, but it was too big. She let out ragged breaths as it was forced into her.

"How does that feel? Does it feel like you are regretting your actions?"

"You already know that I am sorry."

"Oh, it seems like you have a bit of an attitude problem."

With a sharp final push, the dildo was in her, and she let out a cry. Her breath caught in her throat, and her body shook.

"I knew that it would be too much for you. You are weak."

"I got your husband to get me off, does that sound weak?" Isabella hissed, surprising herself.

"You did what?" her voice was livid. "He gave into you?"

Isabella leapt as she was struck with a piece of hard leather. It left her buttocks sore, and her angry. She tensed around the dildo, allowing painful pleasure to flow up through her.

"You are wasting your time." Isabella moaned. "I'm finding this fun."

She could hear her own heavy breaths, and the Mistress pacing about the room. Isabella hadn't meant to speak back to her, but there was something about the taunts that she had to say something. She heard the bedroom door open and close, and then silence.

"Hello?" Isabella called out.

There was no reply. Isabella pulled against the restraints, making her wrists hurt.

"You can't just leave me here!" Isabella said, even though she knew that Elizabeth could.

She imagined the reaction on the faces of any of her co-workers if they found her like this, tied up, with a giant dildo inside her. She kicked at her restraints, knowing that it wouldn't do any good.

Isabella must have fallen asleep, and she was woken by the sound of the door opening. Disorientated, she opened her eyes, unable to see past the blindfold.

"Who is it?" she asked.

"Shhh, it's fine," the Mistress whispered, undoing the buttons on Isabella's dress.

Isabella could tell that there was someone else in the room from the creaking of the floor. She felt the restraints on her ankles being loosened.

She felt Elizabeth's bare skin against her own, as she undid the restraints on Isabella's wrists.

"Are you sorry, Isabella?" she whispered.

"Yes," Isabella murmured, as the Mistress turned her over.

"Good," she could hear the smile in the Mistress' voice, as she reattached the binds to the posts of the bed.

"What are you doing?" Isabella said.

"Since you enjoyed my husband so much earlier, I am going to let you have him again, but on my terms."

The Mistress removed the dildo from Isabella, "You

must be sore from having that in for so long, I'll get you a smaller one."

She left Isabella in suspense yet again. Isabella lay on her back, imagining the master staring at her, taking in her naked and bound body. Once the Mistress had finished choosing a new toy, she drenched it in oil.

"You will love this one, my girl," she hissed, first teasing Isabella's opening with it, letting her feel the cold wetness of the lubricant.

Then she moved it downward, between her buttocks. Isabella tried to resist tensing, as she was caressed by the head of the dildo. Her heart pounded as the Mistress moved it into her. She felt herself gripping onto it hard, as if she was pulling it into herself. Elizabeth had her hand on one of Isabella's hips, keeping her in place. She had gone from a couple of fingers earlier in the evening to a whole dildo, and Isabella steadied her breathing, struggling to cope.

"You're so wet, Isabella," Elizabeth whispered. "I hope you are ready."

"Ready for what?"

"For me, again, Isabella."

She flushed on hearing the master's voice. He was the one who had got her into this situation. Well, maybe they had both got each other into it.

She felt his hard cock at her opening. She already felt so stuffed from the dildo in her ass, she wasn't sure if she could take anything more. The restraints were tight around her wrists, as he eased himself into her, flexing and throbbing. Isabella started to moan, and the Mistress shushed her. Elizabeth climbed onto the bed next to her.

"You cannot be making all that noise."

Before Isabella knew what was happening, her Mistress was on top of her, knees by her head. Isabella had her eyes open, wishing that she could see through the blindfold up at her.

"I'll keep you quiet," the Mistress whispered.

The master had not moved; he was keeping his cock inside her. The Mistress settled down onto Isabella's face.

"Eat up, love, I know you know how."

Isabella kissed her Mistress' clit, feeling it on her tongue. She felt the Mistress tighten her legs around her as she licked and sucked. The master started to thrust into her, holding her legs up from the backs of her thighs, and pushing deep inside. Isabella's head spun, but she knew she had to stay focused on pleasuring her Mistress. Elizabeth rocked back and forth on Isabella's face, wanting her more and harder. Isabella was wide open for both of them, and in no place to resist.

"If you want to be fucked, Isabella," the Mistress laughed, "I can make sure that it happens. But if you go around sneaking behind my back, I will make sure you get fucked so hard you will not be able to walk for a week. It's your choice. Thomas knows that if he goes sneaking around behind my back again that he will get the same, and he will be scrubbing the toilets."

The Mistress pulled the blindfold away from Isabella's eyes. The room was disturbingly bright after being kept in the dark for so many hours. Elizabeth's face settled into view. She smirked on seeing Isabella's reddened face.

Elizabeth lay back on the pillow next to Isabella, and

they looked into each other's eyes, as the master continued to thrust into Isabella.

"I didn't mean to upset you, Mistress," Isabella whispered, her voice jolting with the thrusts.

"I know," the Mistress said, placing one finger on Isabella's lips. "There is one last thing that you need to do."

The master removed himself from Isabella and lay on top of Elizabeth. Isabella felt the sweat and the heat of them. Isabella watched as the Mistress took the master's cock in one hand and guided it into her. She could not take her eyes off them, as they thrusted and moaned together. The bed rocked, as Isabella lay bound and useless.

She's showing me how it feels to be the one who is left out, Isabella thought.

The Mistress glanced from her husband, looking into Isabella's eyes. Their skin trembled against hers. Isabella felt the hot breath on her face, forced from Elizabeth's mouth with each thrust. They both watched the master's face as his moans got louder. He pulled his cock out of her and spilled his cum onto Elizabeth's stomach. Isabella watched with wide eyes.

Elizabeth lay back on the pillow next to her, smiling with red lips. The master released Isabella's wrists, allowing her to sit up. The Mistress brushed Isabella's hair back off her face and pushed her down toward her stomach.

"Lick it up," she whispered.

Isabella put out her tongue and tasted the salty ejaculate, taking it up into her mouth off her Mistress' soft skin. She put her mouth to the Mistress' stomach, sucking up the cum and swallowing it down. The Mistress stroked her hair and the back of her neck.

Isabella dressed back into her floury and sweaty clothes and made her way back to her room.

It would be so easy to act like that if I had loads of money.

She lay in bed, listening to Catherine's snores. Deep down, Isabella knew that money wasn't the only reason she couldn't be like the Mistress. Isabella had tried to leap into something that must have taken years to build up to. The Mistress may have been born rich, but she could not have been born with that strength. Isabella wanted to know how she became this way.

Her journal, Isabella thought. *From her journal I can know her secrets.*

Knowing about the diary was a start, but it still had to be found. She doubted that it would be in the library, but she decided to eliminate it off her list first.

The Mistress was standing on a foot ladder, rearranging books on a high shelf as Isabella let the door close softly behind her. The strong smell of musty books hit her. The Mistress turned and glanced down at her, before rolling her eyes.

"I was not expecting to see you out of your bed so soon."

"And why was that?" Isabella asked, trying to put force into her voice.

"I thought that you would be crying into your pillow, or that you would have run away during the night."

"Run away?"

"Back to wherever you came from, begging mummy and daddy to take their dear slut back."

"I could never go back to my family, and I'm not a slut," Isabella said.

"A slut is a woman who knows what she enjoys, and I have no problem with that. What I do have a problem with is a woman who plays around with other women's husbands without their permission."

The Mistress had begun to leaf through a dusty book.

"You know that I am sorry, and besides, it was him that started it."

"I have decided to forgive you. However, I want you to remember in future that you should not just do things because a man suggests it. It is their world enough, try to claim a bit for yourself. Was there any book you were looking for in particular?"

Isabella felt herself panicking because she had not prepared an answer. "I was—looking for something on local history."

She was happy with that hasty lie, and the Mistress raised an eyebrow.

"I'm impressed, Isabella. How did you know that I find intelligent women so attractive?"

"I didn't think that you would be particularly interested in anyone who couldn't keep up with you."

"True, true." the Mistress smiled, stepping down the ladder. "I was angry at you last night, but it is good to be challenged. I desire you because I sense a kindred spirit. You are a pervert, and that is what I want. You don't want to be fucked for any kind of gain; you want it for sheer pleasure.

And that is how I have always been, I have gained some things, but that has never been the sole reason. I wanted a wealth of experiences, but they were the kind of experiences that high society is always saying is so wrong, unless you are a man, of course.

By now I have done so much, I am sure that few men could compete."

"How did you start?"

"Nosy, Isabella, you want to know how I lost my virginity? I started flirting with the young servants as a teenager. I was never one for seeing them as part of the furniture. An attractive person is attractive regardless of class, and I would never take advantage of anyone. My parents eventually started to scold me for it and tried to introduce me to endless hordes of young men that they thought were suitable. Most of them were red-cheeked, fat men with more land than brain cells. It all stopped once my parents died in a shipwreck when returning from France."

"I am so sorry to hear that."

"You don't have to be. I inherited this house. You didn't think that I had got it from my husband, did you? I was twenty-one at this point, and my parents never had to know that I was not the innocent girl that they were trying to trade away. They knew that I was a flirt, but I would have been on the streets if they ever knew what I had done."

Isabella had one hand on a shelf to balance herself, and the Mistress was looking into the distance, across the long green gardens outside the library window.

"Well, don't stop there," Isabella said.

"I think that it might be another story for another time.

What I did was strange, and not something that you should ever aspire to copy."

The Mistress stepped down the ladder, a distant look still in her eyes. Then Isabella's back was pushed against the ebony shelf, and Elizabeth's lips were on hers, her breath taken away. Her grip was strong on Isabella's shoulder as her tongue flitted into her mouth.

"I guess it's good to be open, sometimes," Elizabeth murmured in a low voice. "I know that I am very closed off. I should remember that no one is coming to take away all that I have achieved."

She pushed an old book with a crumbling spine into Isabella's open hand. "I would recommend this one, though I haven't read it in a while."

Her heart continued to thud as she left the room. Her eyes flitted up and down the table of contents, and she was enticed by a chapter about local traditions, which she decided to look at later in the day. Before that, she was going to continue her search for the journal.

As long as the Mistress was in the library, Isabella was free to look as she liked.

With the book tucked under her arm, she walked up the main staircase. Light flooded through the stained-glass windows ahead of her, casting yellows and reds across the polished wood. Isabella felt safe, the kiss still burnt on her lips, and the stirring in her stomach delighted her. She hoped that she had been forgiven. She trekked down a long corridor to the room from the night before, knowing that it was there that the Mistress must play often.

Her cheeks flushed as she entered the room, trying to

banish thoughts of her punishment from her mind. As she looked through the drawers, she knew that it was going to be unavoidable. She could imagine the gags in her mouth, holding her tongue down, and forcing her to gasp for breath. The braided leather whips were light in her hands and whistled through the air as she swung them. There were many items that Isabella could not recognise, but she felt excited about their use.

The ornate wooden panelling had gone unnoticed when she had been in the room before. She had been far too distracted. Now she paced around, rapping with her knuckles, and to her surprise, a knock turned up a hollow noise. She prised the panel open with her fingernails, and there lay the book that she had been looking for.

Chapter 8

For a moment, Isabella stood in shock, amazed at how easy it had been. She sat down at the desk with it. Out the window, Garrett was exercising one of the horses as several people watched. Even at this distance, she knew that it was him by the flow of his long hair. She started to read.

Virginity is unimportant. Despite what I have been told, it is nothing physical, and I will lose nothing. However, my first time must be worthy of my desires. There have been so many men and women that I could have had. I am twenty-one, there is no need for me to wait. Deep inside, I know that I must make this something worth remembering. I have heard other women speaking in hushed tones about their sexual encounters. Of them being squashed under some man as he thrusts three or four times and it is done. I will never have intercourse that is like that, I will always have something special, something that I deserve and will make happen.

By the next entry, Elizabeth had got what she wanted.

I had known that the wealth that I had been left would come in useful in many ways, but there was one way that I had never dreamed of: bribing a prison officer. For the last month, I have been going as a "lady visitor" to the nearest prison. It's a great imposing building, with four wings, and imagine my delight when I discovered just who they are holding. The condemned man is not supposed to get visitors in his cell, but a bit of money does wonders.

This young man, sentenced to die, was a highwayman. I had seen his posters in the newspaper. Even in the prison uniform, he looked dashing, He had an easy sense of humor, and seemed unafraid. He knew that I was visiting him out of curiosity, and he seemed to find me interesting, Since he was condemned he had two prison officers in the room with him, which made flirtatious conversation all the more exciting. I sat across the small table from him, and I could feel his eyes on me, in my tight bodice. He told me about prison life, and its lack of comforts especially compared to the life that he had led before.

"When I was free," he whispered, "and I had seen a woman like you, I would have loved to tie her up, and relieve her of all of her money."

"And now?"

"I am merely grateful for your company, women are so rare in jail, especially such a beauty." "Have you thought about your final request?" I asked, making his face fall.

"I was thinking about a lot of drink, that's why they call it a hangover." He feigned a laugh.

"I can think of something much, much better."

So, I returned the following week, dressed in all black. I felt like a ghost as I walked through the dark prison. The officers showed me into the cell. The highwayman had been allowed to dress in the clothes that he had been wearing when he was arrested. He lay on the single bed, legs crossed and his arms behind his head. The top buttons of his shirt were undone, he wore long boots and tight trousers. I thought that he looked so out of place in the cell.

"Elizabeth," he said, grinning, "you were late. I was worried that you had changed your mind."

"I would never change my mind."

He stood up and extended a hand out to me. I took it and stole a glance at the prison officers who were sitting in the corner.

"I'm sorry, there's no chance of us getting full privacy," he said. I could tell that he was trying to gauge my reaction.

"I'm still sure that this is what I want to do."

He was slightly taller than me, and as I looked up into his grey eyes, he put his hands around my waist. He was waiting for me to make the first move, to set the pace. I felt daunted, not wanting him to know that I had no experience, other than sneaking kisses in back hallways with servants.

"The world would be better with more women like you," he said, as I started to touch his shoulders.

"What do you mean?"

"You are going out and getting what you want."

"I have advantages that few women have, and I know how lucky I am, so I am not going to let anything stop me."

I started to kiss his neck. He took a gasp of breath. I felt the pound of his heart, and the fine bones around his throat. He pulled the clips from my hair, letting it fall around my shoulders.

"Sit up on the bed, I'm good at something that most men aren't."

The hard springs pressed into me, and the cool wall made me shiver. He got down onto his knees by the bed, and I raised my skirts for him. He ran his hand up my leg, smoothly along my silk stocking. As he took my knickers down, the expectation was becoming too much for me. Here I was, at last. All of the dreaming and desiring in the world would never have prepared me. I shut my eyes to forget the prison officers who sat in the far corner. When his hot mouth was on me, it no longer felt like we were in a jail cell, we could have been in the Sacre Hotel. I clenched around him, and without noticing, I had started to moan and sigh. One of his hands gripped my buttock, the middle finger of his other hand was inside me, where only I had been before. He was my first, and I was his last.

My legs were over his shoulders, and my petticoats rustled as I contorted with the pleasure of it. For someone who had committed such violence, his mouth was gentle, and there was nothing forceful about his hands. It was as if he could sense my years of longing, so he was going to make it last as long as it could. His fingers were getting deeper into me, but I stopped him.

"Undress me with your hands now," I whispered. "Instead of just with your eyes."

He helped me back onto my feet, the room feeling much warmer.

"Such a beautiful choice of fabric," he murmured. "From my experience, I can tell you that many of the wealthy do not choose to dress tastefully. They often wear the kinds of things that I wouldn't even bother to steal. There is very little fun in that. So, I'm not going to fling your clothes on the floor, I'll fold them over the chair instead."

He kept his word and told me of the difficulties of getting a fair deal from your fence if you did not have a good knowledge of the value of the things that you had stolen.

Strangely, I knew that I respected him. He was someone who had made his fortune. It did not all work out for him, but for a while, he had managed to live a life that few of his class could.

He began by unbuttoning my bodice, the tightness of the cloth meant that his hands were on my chest, and I could feel my nipples harden under my stiff corset at his touch.

"I could not have lived through honest means." He sighed. "To be poor and to be honest means a life underpaid in the factories, or toiling for next to nothing in one of the big houses. Always pay your servants well, miss, because few do. And you must wonder yourself if you were born in some back-to-back house in Liverpool, someone beautiful like you, would you accept your lot?"

He exposed my corset and took a deep breath in, his eyes caught by my curves assisted by my tight lacing. He loosened the ties at the back, As an expert, he knew that undoing the clasps first would damage the corset.

"Would you slave away in a factory, destroying your lungs, or would you get on a stage and dance for money? Would you let men pay for your desirable company?"

"I never thought about this," I said, feeling ashamed.

He undid the clasps and cupped my breasts in his hands, running his cool fingers over my nipples.

"Rich men feel the need to destroy everything different. I am a criminal for accidentally killing someone during a robbery, but a factory owner is not a criminal for working women and children into their graves. You are different, Elizabeth." He took my face in his hands. "There are going to be so many rich men who would love to destroy you. They probably wouldn't kill you, *like they are going to do to me. But they would make you marry them, and have children and vapid friends. All your time would be eaten up by dinner parties and risking your life giving birth, and for what? Don't you dare let that happen."*

"I will try my best," I breathed, overwhelmed by the feeling of him touching me, and the intense look that he had in his eyes.

"I'm not always like this." He laughed. "I suppose it's my hanging tomorrow that has me thinking in all kinds of morbid ways, and I feel that I should pass something on."

"I am hoping that I am going to help you feel fulfilled."

"Oh, Elizabeth, I think you will."

I was certainly not underwhelmed by my first sight of a man naked. I sat on the bed, my chest exposed, but still wearing my skirts, as I watched him undress for me. He no longer seemed to care about the presence of the prison officers, who had been trying to avert their eyes. His skin looked lovely in the candlelight, though he had some long and deep scars across his chest and his arms. He did not mention them, so I did not ask. His cock was hard and ready, and I watched as he stroked it with one hand.

"This is insane," I thought, as he started to kiss me again. It felt like my blood was thundering through my veins, and that my body was not big enough, or strong enough to hold back everything that I was feeling. He laid me on my back on the rough sheets, and he lifted the candle from the bedside table, the light showing off his high cheekbones.

"What are you doing?" I murmured.

"Close your eyes, and enjoy it."

I shut my eyes and tried to relax my body. I could feel goosebumps forming across my skin, but from excitement, rather than from the cold air. I leapt in shock as the hot wax dripped onto my chest, and my eyes shot open.

"It feels good, doesn't it?" he said, kneeling over me.

I nodded, and he tilted the candle forward again, allowing the liquid to spill down onto me. I cried out, half in pain and half in pleasure, and I put a hand out to shield myself, but he pushed it away.

"You want more, don't you? This cheap, hot wax, feeling great on your pale and perfect skin?"

"Yes, how can it hurt and feel so good?"

"Because you are strong and powerful, and now you are sometimes going to want people to hurt you."

As he spoke, the candle flickered, a fine line of smoke rose, and the wax hardened as it hit me. I flinched and tensed. I had thought that clothes helped people to feel powerful, but at that moment I realised that it was all about attitude. He did not feel any need to shy away from me.

I watched him set the candle back down, and he peeled away the wax from my chest, the skin tender from the burning.

"You are going to take over from here." He smiled. "This was your idea, and I'm going to be grateful for this forever, no matter where I end up going. I'm sure that you have plenty of plans in that lovely head of how you wanted tonight to go, so let me help those dreams come true."

I felt myself flushing, which I knew was stupid of me. Of course, he would know that I had had decadent thoughts, and it was far too late to feel ashamed.

"It doesn't have to be anything too crazy, you can save that for other lucky people."

I could not help but laugh; he had such high hopes for my future.

"I know that I want to be on top of you."

"Of course!" he said as he lay down on the bed next to me.

It was a slim, single bed, so there was not too much space. I kept a hand to the wall as I straddled him. He was grinning, and I pulled my skirts up around my hips, our thighs touched, and I felt the hardness of his perfect cock press against me. I wriggled about on top of him, as he used one hand to guide himself into me. The head pressed into the wetness of my opening, and the lips parted. He pushed up into me, I gasped, and my eyes threatened to roll back into my skull.

"I really, really want to draw this out," he murmured, already sounding short of breath. "But the feeling of how tight you are around me, and the sight of you is making me feel so weak."

I rocked my hips forward once, sliding his cock the whole way into me, and he let out a long sigh. I was having more difficulty expressing myself. He put both of his hands on my buttocks.

"Please, more."

I made large circles with my hips, turning and turning. I felt his cock throb deep in me as it caressed my walls. His head was thrown back, his hands gripping me tighter and tighter. I had heard other girls whisper of the pains of the first time that they had been fucked, but I was not feeling that at all. Though my first time was so extremely different to that of other girls of my class. This was not my wedding night, I would never see this man again. We were not on a four-poster bed in some expensive hotel. And I was not doing my wifely duty by lying still and taking it. The fact that this was so different and so wrong, was just serving to make me feel even more turned on. All the rules of society that I had been taught were being ripped to shreds by each thrust of my hips.

I moved into a crouching position, my feet on either side of his hips. He put his warm hands on the small of my back to support me. I began to bounce on his cock, and as I would land down hard on him, he would thrust up into me. I started to touch my clit, stirring dark and animal feelings inside myself, and hot moans of pleasure erupted from me. His eyes were glinting as he gripped my hips tighter, and his thrusts and mine became faster and harder.

"I think we should try to be a bit quieter," he hissed. "I wouldn't want to attract any unwanted attention."

"I don't know if I can!" I cried.

He held me by the hips to still me, and slowly pulled his cock out of me, wet with my pleasure.

"What are you doing?" I asked, lying down beside him.

"You'll see."

He drew one of my legs up, unbuckling my shoe. He started to caress my toes through the silk stocking, and then the sensitive sole of my foot, making me laugh. He worked his hand up my leg, my firm calf, the back of my knee. He stroked my thigh through the lace at the top of my stocking, before unclipping it and rolling it down my leg.

"What do you need..." I began to ask, but before I had the chance to finish my sentence, he had gagged me with my stocking.

He tied it tightly behind my head and smiled. "I think that will help."

I opened my legs, my mouth dry around the gag as I breathed heavily.

"Do you want this?"

I nodded furiously.

Without a pause, he was back inside of me, and I held his firm buttocks, pushing him deep in. I could feel all his weight on top of me, his hot breath on my neck. His touch told me of his endless experience, and I bit down hard on the stocking, feeling the fabric tear. He was pounding into me, and as he kissed my neck, I gasped for breath. I felt as though I were floating, and that my body would never experience something so amazing and beautiful ever again.

Then it happened, my first orgasm in front of another person, and I cried out into my gag as he bit me.

He buried his face in a handful of my hair, and I felt a hot rush deep inside as he came as well.

My heart was still pounding as he helped me put my clothes back on. I gripped his hand as I was shown to the cell door.

"Thank you so much, Elizabeth," he murmured, kissing my hand.

I took a last glimpse of his handsome face as the door clanked shut, and he was gone from me forever. The sound of my footsteps seemed so loud in the darkened jail, so I tried to walk on my toes. I could hear muttering voices behind the cell doors, and I was unsure if the prisoners were talking to themselves or someone else. A place like that would be a test of any person's sanity, the same rooms, and the same faces for years and years. I will not let my world become my jail. I will always have my freedom.

Isabella turned over the page to find a newspaper article about the highwayman. A picture of him made him look cocky and confident. She could see why the Mistress wanted him. Isabella stuffed the journal away and sat down. She felt lightheaded and in serious need of a cup of strong tea. She had seen something of herself in the younger version of the Mistress. She already felt that she had learnt a huge lesson. She did not need money or a huge amount of experience. What she needed was to keep a hold on her freedom, and to do whatever it takes to live her dream life, no matter who says it is wrong.

Chapter 9

With a cup of tea and some toast, Isabella retreated to her room. Catherine would be out doing her cleaning duties, and Isabella knew that she should be helping her. She was still shaking with nerves. She could not get the image of her Mistress and the highwayman out of her head. Elizabeth must always have been a force of nature, even when she had no experience. A woman like that would be hard to keep interested. She shook the thoughts from her head and lifted the book that she had borrowed from the library. The cover was dark, worn leather. The Mistress had seemed so charmed when Isabella showed interest in the book, and she knew that she had to read it. She wanted the Mistress to think of her as an equal, and this would help her to seem more cultured.

The spine creaked as she opened it, and she turned to the chapter on local festivals in the hope of finding something fun. Most of them were of the dull and religious variety, and she hastily skipped over them; she didn't want to be reminded of what she had escaped from. She wanted to find something pagan and human, something that had been forgotten about for hundreds of years. Then she saw it, the Festival of Rota Fortunae, The Festival of the Wheel of Fortune. It was a Medieval Summer Festival. A woodcut print on the page showed an image of a blindfolded woman holding the wheel, ladies, peasants and knights clung to the wheel. For one day, the high could be brought low, and the low could be raised up. The book mentioned lords and ladies mucking out stables, repairing their servants' clothes, and the peasants not having to work at all, instead spending their day at play. Isabella's breath caught in her throat; this day would be exactly the kind of thing that she would love to experience.

She was so caught up in reading, that she was startled by Catherine entering the room.

"I wasn't expecting you to be here," Catherine said. "I haven't seen you awake since the dance, you didn't seem to notice me at all that night."

"I'm sorry, a lot was going on that night, it was all so new to me."

"You will get used to them." She sighed. "I am more than used to all these grand dances and balls. Working at them, I mean, never as a guest, not like you."

Isabella picked up the bitterness in the other girl's voice and felt ashamed of herself for not trying harder to seek her out.

"Catherine, I'm still just like you. I have been lucky to get the Mistress' favor, but we are still the same!"

"I'm not sure if I wish to be the same as you or not, Isabella! I have to get up early and work away while you sleep. You get in no trouble for not working, but at what cost to yourself?"

"There is no cost!"

"If people find out about this, you will be the talk of the county."

"I will not, no one cares about what a servant girl gets up to. I'll help you out for a while, but can we please just drop the subject?"

They cleaned together in silence. Isabella caught Catherine staring out of the window, her expression blank. Isabella knew that Catherine was thinking about something. Isabella knew that something like this was going to happen, the Mistress treated her differently from the rest of the servants, so of course, the servants were going to treat her differently too. What she saw in Catherine was not jealousy, but genuine fear and concern.

It was a relief to get away from her, the stiff silence was stressing her, and making her feel as if she did have something to worry about. She sat outside on one of the metal benches, with views toward the lawns. It was difficult to get comfortable in her stiff uniform. She could see that Garrett was out with one of the horses again. He was leading a tall chestnut horse, and the Mistress was sitting confidently on the horse's back. Garrett was laughing at something she said. He looked comfortable around her. Isabella had not seen the Mistress with the other servants very often, but from what she had seen, they were respectful to her to an extreme, and would only speak when spoken to.

The Mistress swung her leg forward, allowing Garrett to tighten the horse's girth. Her leg was against his shoulder, and Isabella felt something tighten deep in her stomach, a twinge of jealousy and confusion. The Mistress and Garrett looked beautiful together. He was carefree and just a little bit dirty, mud high on his tall boots, his shirt untucked, and he swept back his long hair with one hand. The Mistress looked as perfect as ever, her long hair was swept up under a small hat, which sat at a rakish angle on her head. She wore a dark blue riding coat, and she sat side-saddle on the horse. Isabella supposed that she was in a complicated situation with both of these gorgeous people, and hopefully, neither of them knew about it.

The Mistress encouraged the horse to trot away from Garrett, around in a circle, and then cantered in the direction of Isabella. She pulled up ahead of her with a smile on her face, a curl had escaped from her tight hairstyle and tickled her nose.

"You are out here looking terribly gloomy!" the Mistress called to her, moving in closer.

"That's just my face!" Isabella called back, hoping Garrett was far enough away so he wouldn't overhear.

"I know that is not true," the Mistress replied with a smug smile. "Have you finished the book yet? Do you want any more recommendations?"

"Oh, you'll have to give me more time, I am meant to be working here as well."

Isabella was desperately trying not to think about the Mistress' journal, which had been far more interesting.

"I know." The Mistress sighed. "I work you far too hard, you must deserve a little holiday."

"I have read some of the book. I was reading about local traditions and festivals."

"Anything exciting that we still do?"

"Not particularly, but I found one, that has fallen out of favor, but maybe it would be fun to try?"

"What is it?"

Isabella explained about the festival, the Mistress narrowed her eyes in thought, unsure.

"It would just be for one day, and it would be a bit different. I know how much you love parties and dressing up."

"I would look very odd in a uniform like yours, would I not?"

"We won't know until we see."

"How would we decide the lord and lady of the mansion for the day?"

"I think it should be the two newest servants."

"That would be you, and our handsome stable boy, wouldn't it?"

"I think it would be."

The Mistress turned to face the park where Garrett was standing watching. She stroked the neck of the horse, who whickered softly. Isabella could feel the hot breath of the horse on her face, smelling of hay and dampness.

"He is a great horseman, and certainly easy enough to look at."

"So do you think we could have this festival?"

"I'll send some letters out, and see if any of my friends would be interested in taking part."

Chapter 10

Isabella was a servant with a huge secret so big that it made her shiver with excitement even thinking about it. She had to conceal that she had the favor of the Mistress and their relationship. Isabella had to trust Catherine to keep her secret, and in return, Isabella shared her presents of chocolates and perfumes with her. The bribes helped to keep her sweet when Isabella was sneaking back into their room late at night.

"I love seeing you dressed like that, and knowing what's underneath," the Mistress murmured into Isabella's ear one evening.

The Mistress had an affection for Isabella's uniform and made sure that she was always dressed perfectly.

Isabella set a tray of drinks that she had been carrying on the end table by the four-poster bed. They were in the main bedroom; the master was with some friends in the smoking room in the other end of the house.

parents were coping, if they had hired someone to replace their overworked daughter, or if their tightness with money had caused them to take all of Isabella's work on themselves. When she thought about it, that was what she hoped for, because then they would understand how hard they had made her work, and without pay.

She had been so caught up in her bitterness that she had barely noticed the Mistress starting to undress her, the apron tossed in a heap on the floor.

"I was thinking about how much I love this frilled shirt on you, should I get you a little hat to match it?"

"I would love it if you didn't."

The overdress came off easily, leaving Isabella in her shirt and petticoat.

"So many layers, it's like unwrapping a present," the Mistress murmured, her eyes glinting and bright as she undid the dark buttons on Isabella's shirt.

She led Isabella through into the dressing room, and Isabella saw the exercise machine. It did not look very much like a horse. Instead of legs, it had an engine, a large saddle on top of it. Instead of a head and reins, it had two long handles.

"I think I prefer the look of real horses. They look much friendlier than…this."

"Friendliness is not the purpose. Now slip out of your knickers and get on."

Isabella took her shift off over her head, and pulled her knickers down, giving her Mistress a wink. She climbed onto the strange horse, gripping the handles, and sat into the firm leather saddle.

"I got the saddle to be made twice as big, to suit our purposes," the Mistress said, flicking a switch on the machine, a low rumbling began. "I'll let you enjoy it for a bit first, and then I will join you."

The Mistress leaned back into a chair, her dressing gown falling softly open, teasing Isabella with a quick glimpse of her pale body, the dark hollow between her breasts. Isabella could feel the vibrations deep inside the machine, moving upward and growing stronger. The seat began to move up and down, and she gripped the handles hard.

"So that's what it does," the Mistress said, lighting a cigarette and taking a deep drag.

Without any kind of warning, Isabella let out an involuntary moan. She tilted her body forward, pushing her clitoris into the saddle, and letting the vibrations hammer against her. She felt herself tighten and tense, a rush of intense pleasure surging inside her. The feelings were so strong that she had trouble keeping her eyes open.

"I don't want you to finish before I have a chance to enjoy you." The Mistress laughed.

She dropped her gown onto the seat, and she lifted a silk-covered object from a shelf.

She hitched up her dressing gown and climbed onto the saddle with Isabella, who could see that she was wearing nothing underneath. They sat facing each other. The Mistress clasped her legs around Isabella, and she leaned back, exposing the perfect red hair between her legs.

"Fuck me with this, would you?" The Mistress moaned,

handing her a silk-covered object. She unwrapped it to find a shining leather dildo. "Wet it with your mouth first."

Isabella opened wide and welcomed it in, running her tongue over the extensive length and girth, gagging as she took it as deeply as she could. It came out glistening with her spit. The vibrations rumbled deep in her, as the Mistress moved and opened her legs. With one hand, Isabella spread her lips, exposing her, pink and wet. The dildo was long, with a curved end. She nuzzled the head between the parted lips, touching the opening. The beautiful combination of Isabella's spit and the wetness of her Mistress allowed Isabella to slide the full length of it.

"Fuck me, please," the Mistress moaned.

She felt the Mistress dig her sharp nails into her back, shutting her eyes tight and opening her mouth. Isabella leaned into her, feeling her hot breath on her face. Her legs were over Isabella's and wrapped tighter around her waist. She slid the dildo out, almost the whole way. the Mistress tilted her head back, eyelids fluttering. Isabella slid it back in, feeling herself getting wetter and more frustrated, as the vibrations echoed through her body, and watching the Mistress bite her perfect, plump lower lip, as she was filled with the imitation cock.

Isabella gripped onto the saddle tighter with her legs; she had never felt anything like it. The silk nightgown was as thin as a sheet of paper, and she used her free hand to explore the body of her beautiful Mistress. Isabella felt her Mistress breathing harder and harder. Her nipples stood out through the fabric. Isabella gripped the dildo, feeling her Mistress' wetness.

She reached down the front of the Mistress' silk nightdress, skimming her fingers over the hard nipple.

"Ah, so cold," she murmured, her breaths short and disjointed.

Isabella pinched the nipple between her fingers, still working hard with her other hand. Isabella found herself grinding against her own hand and the wrong end of the dildo. The movements of the horse made her stomach lurch. She was taken by surprise, as the Mistress bit her as she orgasmed. Her perfect white teeth were painful and brilliant on Isabella's neck. Her legs wrapped so tight around her waist, pushing the breath out of her. She was biting so hard that she drew a thin sliver of blood from Isabella.

The Mistress unwrapped herself from Isabella, and Isabella felt her stomach sink, sure that the fun was over and that she was going to be sent back to her room. Instead, the Mistress switched the machine off, and it ground to a halt. The room was still except for the sounds of their heavy breathing.

"Did you like that?" Elizabeth murmured.

"I did."

"Then we should do that again sometime."

Isabella looked at Elizabeth and wondered how obvious her longing was. The redness in her cheeks and lips, the hardness of her nipples, and the way she crossed her legs, thighs tight together.

The Mistress had stepped toward her, her mouth open and a thoughtful look in her eyes. She scooped Isabella up into her arms with one arm under her knees and the other at the small of her back, surprising her. Isabella draped her arms around her neck and laughed.

She was carried through into the bedroom and set down on the silk sheets of her Mistress' bed.

Isabella opened her legs eagerly, as the Mistress placed one hand on her thigh.

"I have figured out how we can do the festival, the wheel of fortune festival." The Mistress smiled.

As much as Isabella was excited to hear this, she was also hoping that the Mistress was going to help her get off.

"It is going to be so much fun, Isabella, I promise!"

"Please tell me about it."

"So, I think that it should last a day and a night, and I will play at being a servant to you, I will invite all of my most exciting friends to do the same. You and that handsome new servant will be the lord and lady of the mansion."

"Do you mean Garrett?"

"Yes, I do, you would be happy with that, wouldn't you? Since people might find out about this, it's better that I do not pair you with someone of the…fairer sex."

"I understand that."

"I am glad that works for you, let me help you dress."

Isabella tried not to let the irritation show in her face as the Mistress helped her back into her clothes. Her Mistress must have known what she was doing to her when she did that. Isabella was burning up with frustration and desire.

She stormed down the corridor, her nails digging into her palms. The gas lamps on the walls hissed, as they were turned down for the night.

She changed into her night chemise and got into bed.

She lay there and stared up at the ceiling. The house was quiet, and she could hear her roommate snoring softly. She knew what she had to do to make herself less annoyed. Under the sheets, she pulled up her chemise and stretched out her bare legs. She was not wearing anything underneath it. This reminded her of nights at home, after a strenuous day of prayer, cleaning and hating her life. She would pull out her box of dirty stories, and by candlelight, she would read, and she would improve her mood.

On this night, she had nothing to read. Instead, she had to rely on her imagination, and trust herself to be quiet enough.

Chapter 11

By the time she woke up, Isabella was in her room on her own. Her mood was still slightly sour from the night before. She looked out the window toward the lawns and decided that a walk outside might be what she needed to clear her head. She wanted to dress in something that was not her uniform, and picked out a light printed cotton dress, not wanting to attract too much attention.

The stables were quiet when she entered, other than the snorting of the horses, and the rhythm of brushing. She glanced over the doors to see if she could find him. The horses looked sleek and well-rested, and she wondered if she would ever be able to learn to ride.

She found Garrett, bent over, facing away from her, brushing out the tail of a bay horse. His thighs looked strong and muscular in his tight jodhpurs. He heard her come in and glanced up. When he realised it was her, he hastily struggled to his feet. She leaned both her arms on the wooden door and smiled at him.

"Good morning, Garrett."

"This is a lovely surprise, Miss Isabella."

He raised an eyebrow and smiled, meaning she could not tell if he was being genuine or not.

"I have something to tell you."

A look of concern darted across his face. If she had blinked in that second, she would have missed it. She tried to ignore it.

"What is it?" he asked, trying to sound casual.

"Well, the master and Mistress want to throw this old-fashioned festival, where places are swapped, and they've picked us to be the master and Mistress for a day."

"What? Why do they want to do that, and why us?"

"Because we are the newest to start working here. Why do you look so worried? It will be fun, I'm sure!"

Garrett turned back to the horse and started to brush again. "I don't know, Isabella, maybe you should ask someone else. It's not really my kind of thing."

"What?" she stuttered. "But...I...they really want you to take part. Everyone is taking part!"

"I'm not meant for those sorts of fancy rooms, playing at being some kind of stuffy lord. I'm free out here, I love my space, I have my work, and people leave me alone."

"People? I think you are being stubborn and no fun!"

"Depends on what you find fun, doesn't it? I'm not like you, I don't want to be the centre of attention. I'm happy to see you feeling more confident and excited about life, compared to how you were when we first met, but I'm not going to let life at this big house change me. I will sleep above the stables, even though the Mistress has offered me this lovely bedroom in the house."

"She's been down here? And she offered you a room?"

"Yes."

"And she came down here to talk to you?"

"Yes, much like how you come down. Why is that strange to you? Sure, she is pleasant to you as well. I've heard that you barely do a tap of work and she never complains."

"You never seem to be working too hard yourself! Every time that I see you, you are patting the horses or trotting some show horse about the lawns!"

He laughed. "I'm not criticising you for not doing any work. This job is a gift. I get to show off and ride the most beautiful horses and explore the grounds. I think you'd like it if you took a bit more of a look around. There are waterfalls, little ruins, and summer houses.

Can you ride?"

"No, my family didn't think that it was appropriate."

"Well, you're away from all that now, and there's no time like the present."

He opened the door of the stall, and she watched him as he put the tack onto two of the horses. His hands were gentle, and the animals seemed to trust him. She felt a bit nervous around horses, with their impatient, pacing feet, and their strangely intelligent eyes.

Garrett had put a side-saddle onto one of the horses, and she followed him at a distance as he led the two great beasts out into the courtyard.

"I'll be on Bracken, and you will be on Captain George," Garrett said.

Isabella eyed the grey horse, deciding whether they were going to be friends or not.

"He's so sweet and gentle. Say hello to him."

Garrett took Isabella's gloved hand and guided it toward Captain George's soft nose, and she glanced up at him, to make sure that she was doing it right.

"So, you've never been on a horse before?"

"No."

"And nothing like a horse? Not even a donkey at the seaside?"

Isabella's mind flashed to the mechanical horse, and she could also feel Elizabeth's hot breath on her face. She banished the thought and looked up at him. She was so close that she could see the scatter of freckles on his straight nose. He couldn't know about the mechanical horse. Could he?

"No, nothing like a horse, I've never even been to the seaside."

"You'll be fine, let's get you up on his back."

She felt a sinking in her stomach as she saw how high up the saddle was.

"Grip the front and back, bend your knee, and I'll give you a leg up."

She felt him grip her calf through her thin dress, and before she had time to think too much about it, he had thrown her up onto the back of the horse. She tried to arrange herself neatly, one leg around the pommel, and her dress flowing behind her, just like the pictures that she had seen in magazines.

"You're a natural horsewoman," Garrett smiled. His teeth were a brilliant white against the tan of his skin.

She liked the feel of his hands as he arranged the reins

for her. How his hands could be so callused and yet so gentle surprised her, and it reminded her of her own when she had to work hard as well.

"That's it," he said, as she gripped the reins between her ring and small fingers.

He seemed like a completely different person when he was talking about the horses, and she found his enthusiasm a bit infectious. With no effort, he was able to jump up into the saddle of his horse.

"All ready to go?"

The horse took long strides, and Isabella gripped tighter with her legs out of fear. Garrett was talking about the plants and wildlife on the grounds. Isabella had no idea what he was talking about, but his passion made his eyes light up as he glanced around at her. She was struck again by how attractive she found him. They sauntered along one of the wood-lined paths, Captain George following Bracken without question.

They dismounted at the trickling waterfall, and Isabella stood looking at it, relishing in the sunlight.

"Come and sit down," Garrett said, as he sat on one of the smooth rocks by the pool.

"I just know that your legs are going to be sore tomorrow."

She sat next to him, their knees almost touching. He pushed a strand of hair behind his ear.

"Are you glad that you ran away, Isabella?" he whispered.

She glanced over at him; he wasn't accusing her of anything.

"Your secret is safe with me," he said. "I'm the only one who knows."

"Of course, I'm glad. I would never have got to do anything like this."

"What? Ride a horse? Sit by a waterfall in the sunlight? Or be alone with a man?"

She didn't want to tell him that she had been alone with a man before, and that men weren't the only ones to be cautious of. "It's almost lunchtime, I'm sure people will be wondering where I am."

He stood silently next to her after helping her back onto the horse, watching the splashing water.

"I'll do it, Isabella."

"Do what?"

"I'll be in your stupid festival."

Great, she thought, *I win.*

She walked into the house, feeling a bit smug. She pulled a piece of straw off her skirt and felt her stomach rumble.

To the kitchens, I suppose, she thought with a shrug.

There were murmurs of The Festival of the Wheel of Fortune all around the servants' quarters. One of the cooks cornered Isabella in one of the corridors.

"So, I've heard this festival was your suggestion," the woman said, jabbing a chubby finger at her. "Of all the old festivals to bring back, why did you have to choose this one? Couldn't we have brought back the football matches where the whole town plays?"

"Or," someone else butted in, "we could have greased up a pig and chased it around the town."

"Oh, that always sounded liked the best."

Isabella knew that there was nothing that she could say that would convince them that her idea was better. They would never understand how Isabella would feel with the Mistress at her feet, doing her will.

"Look," Isabella said, standing her ground, "I know you all have things in mind that you would like to be doing, but I was the one who managed to suggest something!"

That made the cook roll her eyes at her.

"But!" Isabella said, trying to inject as much enthusiasm into her voice as possible.

"It's going to be so fun for all of us! The Mistress—"

"Oh, the Mistress!" One of the maids laughed, doing a bad impression of Isabella's voice.

"The Mistress," Isabella continued, she wouldn't be shaken that easily, "is having a group of her friends over, and they are going to be serving us! And the rules dictate that we can get in no trouble for how we treat our 'servants', within reason, of course, we are all meant to be having fun."

The cook folded her arms. "Not having to work for a day does sound good, I suppose."

Isabella smiled.

"They are all going to be so pathetic." One of the maids laughed. "Finally, they will realise how hard our job really is!"

Everyone in the house was annoyed to be making

preparations for the friends to be arriving, making up beds, making sure there was enough food. All of it had to be done to make sure that the festival could run as smoothly as possible.

The Mistress hadn't called Isabella to her in days, too busy, Isabella supposed. In whatever time she had free, she would watch the carts and carriages coming up the tree-lined lane to the house, delivering parcels and people.

"I'm hoping it's everything that you want it to be, Isabella," Catherine said cautiously.

"I hope so too."

"I've been told you have just one more thing to do, then you are your own Mistress for a day."

"Huh?"

"I was told to fetch you, for a drawing."

"A drawing?"

"That's all I was told. I was told to get you and my drawing kit."

She picked up her case and her sheaf of papers.

"Come on, Isabella, down to the library."

The house was still, but Isabella imagined that she could feel a sense of anticipation in the building, like a trembling in the floorboards. Isabella felt deep down that after the next few days things wouldn't be quite the same again. The lamps were turned down, so she struggled to see, and had to watch her step as she walked down the stairs.

Ahead of the door, she could see Elizabeth's pale face glowing in the moonlight. She looked as if she came from another planet, her eyes were impossible to read. "There she is," the Mistress whispered. "Our model for this evening."

"Our?" Isabella murmured.

"Go on into the library, Catherine, I will get Isabella ready."

Elizabeth turned her away as Catherine opened the door.

"I wanted to have things my way, one last time before the festival." Elizabeth said with a smile.

"It's only for a day."

"I have never had a day where I wasn't in command."

Isabella thought that she could see some nervousness in her Mistress' bright eyes; the look didn't suit her. Within a second, her face had turned back to normal.

"I need you to take your clothes off, Isabella."

"What? Out here? Can't we go to your room?"

"It is for the drawing, and there's no one about. Put this on after."

She hadn't noticed that Elizabeth was holding a dark and silky gown. She placed it on the door handle.

"I never get to wear clothes around you, do I?" Isabella smirked, making the Mistress snort. "All those pretty dresses you've given me, that you never let me wear."

"I love to see them on you, of course. I love seeing you walk about in the finery I've given you, seeing how well it suits you." She had unbuttoned the bodice and slid it off her shoulders, and she let the skirt fall around her ankles. "Tonight, I am going to make a goddess of you."

Her lips were so close, and the urgency with which she was removing her clothes had Isabella wishing that she would push her up against the wall and kiss her, but she was nervous about anyone seeing them.

The Mistress piled up Isabella's clothes. Isabella felt her nipples harden in the cool air.

The Mistress put the cold silk around her shoulders and clinched it at the waist with the tie.

"Such a pity to cover you up." She said, grinning and opening the door into the library.

Isabella jumped in shock when she realised that there were several people already in there. All of them were women, seated with easels, including Catherine, who gasped when she saw Isabella in the translucent, knee-skimming gown.

"Here is our beautiful model for tonight, Miss Isabella."

There were murmurs of approval from the seated women. The Mistress' hand was on Isabella's shoulder, stopping her from backing out of the room. A raised area had been set up, on it a chaise lounge and a curtain backdrop. The five women behind their easels stared as the Mistress escorted Isabella up onto the platform.

"You should have told me about this!" Isabella hissed.

"Would you have agreed if I had asked?"

Isabella spluttered an unsure response as the robe was whisked off her, and draped over the chaise lounge.

"Lie down for me."

With the Mistress' back to them, the painters couldn't see her eyes all over their model. She arranged her, one arm draped over her bed, a rose between her fingers, lying on her side, facing toward the potential artists.

"Wonderful," the Mistress murmured.

Isabella tried to keep her breathing steady; she had never been naked in front of this many people before.

Having a hoard of eyes watch as her Mistress' delicate hand moved a lock of hair to drape over her collar bone, and down over her breast. Her index finger lingered on her hard nipple, Isabella felt her heart thud, so loud that she was sure that Elizabeth could hear it.

"Now," the Mistress said, stepping back to admire her arrangement, "we can't expect Miss Isabella to wait around all night, so we had better get started."

She sat down and started to sharpen a pencil with a knife, the blade peeling away a long curl of wood, revealing the sharpened lead. Isabella heard the scratching of pencils on paper, and she started to relax more. She watched the Mistress' expression of deep concentration, her tongue pushing out over the edge of her full lip. She caught her eyes, and they smiled at each other, their connection secret and electric, making her breath catch in her throat. How well the Mistress could pretend that she had never seen Isabella's naked body before. Her roommate, Catherine, on the other hand, tried to look at Isabella as little as she possibly could, making hasty scribbles on her paper. Isabella and Catherine were the only ones not decorated in jewels and beautiful clothes. Everyone else had glittering gems dripped off them. Catherine glanced up, reddening as she realised that Isabella was looking at her. She furrowed her brow; Isabella liked that. She let the women take in every inch of her body, and attempt to replicate it on paper, from the hard skin on the bottom of her feet, that she was a bit ashamed of, her firm calves, her round hips, all the way up to her delicate collarbones and her dark hair.

The Mistress took out her pocket watch and

encouraged everyone to finish up. Isabella put the robe back around her shoulders. The drawings were of varying quality, ranging from a crude sketch by one of the unfamiliar women, to the intricate sketch that the Mistress had created. Lastly, she looked at Catherine's drawing. She felt a tightening in her chest looking at it. She thought that it was so lovely. She had drawn her lips and the rose the same color, a confident look on her face.

"Is that how you see me?" Isabella murmured.

"I would like to finish it properly at some point, if you wouldn't mind posing again,"

Catherine said, reddening once more.

"Of course," Isabella smiled.

"We should be getting to bed now," the Mistress announced. "We all have a big day ahead of us tomorrow."

She and Isabella waited as the people filtered out of the room, muttering to each other.

Isabella watched Catherine leave, clutching her drawing to her chest.

"Did you have fun, Isabella?" the Mistress asked once they were alone.

"Yes, but you still should have told me."

"And why is that?"

"I could have been on my period!"

Chapter 12

Isabella slept fitfully, nervous and excited for the festival. Her idea! She was going to be the Mistress of Mordancross House! Even if it was only for a day! Catherine was already asleep by the time she got back to the room; the drawing of Isabella was already safely stowed away.

Isabella woke up later than usual, a gentle hand on her shoulder.

"Apologies for the lateness, my Mistress," a quiet voice whispered.

Isabella opened her eyes, wondering who this could be. To her surprise, the demure voice belonged to her Mistress. Her red hair was piled up on her head, in a bun, a few strands escaping and curling on her cheeks. She was dressed in a perfectly fitted maid's uniform of a long black dress and a dainty white apron.

"Come with me to get dressed."

Catherine giggled in disbelief and waved to Isabella as she followed Elizabeth to her bedroom.

"I must apologise again for my lateness," Elizabeth whispered, glancing downward.

"It was not a good impression to make as your new maid."

Isabella couldn't help but laugh; she was a good actress. She sat on Elizabeth's bed as her maid picked out an outfit for her to wear.

Isabella stood in her chemise and drawers as Elizabeth laced her into her corset.

"Your fingers feel wonderful, Elizabeth." Isabella sighed, wondering when would be too soon to flirt with her.

Elizabeth reddened, and Isabella wondered how she could do that on command; she seemed to be quite the actress.

Isabella turned to face her, admiring how the tie of her apron highlighted her slim waist. Black and white looked good on Elizabeth, making her red hair look like fire. Isabella ran a finger along her cheek, and felt her take a breath in, and leaned in to kiss her. Elizabeth stepped away.

"I want to kiss you."

"Me? Mistress Isabella? What would everyone say if they knew?"

Isabella rolled her eyes. *She plays a sweet girl well, and she's managing to tease me. I would feel creepy if I didn't know what she is really like.*

There was a knock at the door, and the master, now dressed as a manservant, stepped in with Garrett, who looked out of place in a fine suit and wing collared shirt. He instantly flushed when he saw Isabella barely dressed, and he turned to leave.

"Why would master Garrett be trying to leave his lady?" the master smiled, showing who was actually in control out of the two of them.

Garrett shot Isabella an accusing look and let go of the door handle. Compared to the previous night, she felt pretty well dressed.

Garrett watched as Elizabeth dressed her. Isabella was unsure of how to act. Play innocent? Show off a little? She made little sighs as her corset was tightened, glancing over at him as she did. Elizabeth didn't give away how she was feeling.

Isabella sat down for Elizabeth to dress her hair and finish up. She had never had anyone else put her hair up, and she knew that she could easily get used to it. She draped a necklace of silver and sapphires around her neck, making her smile as she looked back at herself in the mirror. The dress was light cotton, but a beautiful silver and blue print, perfect for a little bit of sport.

The dining room had an excited atmosphere. All the servants in the house were dressed up in clothes that were not their own. They looked fresh and relaxed from sleeping in, and not having to prepare their food.

The master and Mistress, and their friends, fussed around the table, making sure that everyone had enough to eat and enough tea to drink. Isabella and Garrett sat at the head of the table. As he watched their new servants scurry around, she thought about how odd he looked in those clothes. The cravat was tied just a bit too tight around his neck, and even though his coat and trousers hugged his frame temptingly, it looked out of place on him. Maybe he was right about not belonging in this world.

"Look how happy everyone is." She said, smiling.

"Relieved that your odd plan is paying off?" He asked.

"Of course, after how some people reacted to the idea."

"Everyone is happy because they actually appreciate someone doing something for them. Not like these rich people. They were born expecting servants to wait on them hand and foot."

"Is it wrong to enjoy it?"

"No, it's understandable, but the best life would be one where I'm nobody's servant and nobody's master."

"I guess, I don't think I'd like someone dressing me every morning."

"I know, it's better to have someone undress you every night." He said, blushing. "Sorry, I don't know why I said that."

She laughed at his concerned expression.

After breakfast, they were taken out to the front lawn to play croquet. Isabella teamed up with Catherine.

"I have no idea how to play, but that doesn't make me any less competitive!"

Catherine spat, picking up one of the bats.

"I didn't figure you to be the competitive type," Isabella said.

Isabella was reduced to tears laughing, over and over, as she chased after the ball, exhausting herself. The heels of her shoes sank into the grass, and she almost tripped. Later, they picked strawberries from the bushes and sat in the shade to eat them. Isabella wished that it could last forever, but the clouds darkened, and specks of rain started to fall, forcing them back inside, to prepare for dinner.

Isabella had to dress herself, as all the upper-class servants were away preparing the many courses.

She was struggling with the back of a red silk dress. She rolled her eyes. It was so frustrating that all the most exquisite clothes were designed to have someone else dress you, to show off that you could afford that. As she was reaching around, looking in the mirror, Catherine stepped into the room, looking a bit ashamed.

"I'm glad to see that you are having the same problem." Catherine laughed.

Isabella turned her back to her, to allow her to button her in, tightening her dress to her body. Catherine turned to allow her to do the same. She looked so different, all dressed up. Catherine still favored dark colors.

"Are you enjoying yourself?" Isabella asked.

"Of course, but it's making me wish that I never had to work so that I could spend more time on my art."

"I know." Isabella sighed. "Imagine how talented we would be."

There was a knock at the door, and Catherine answered it. There Garrett stood wearing a tailcoat, still looking a bit out of place. Isabella wished she could change him back into a loose shirt and his high boots.

"I'm here to escort you ladies to dinner." He smiled.

Isabella was on his right and Catherine on the left, as they made their way down the main staircase. The light from the stained-glass window was warm on her back, and it cast a rainbow of colours over the stairs.

Someone, who must have been a friend of the master, dressed in a dark uniform, opened the door into the dining room for them.

Isabella sat at the head of the table, sipping a glass of expensive wine as the food started to be brought in. The room was long and narrow, the dining table, lined with chairs in the centre of the room. The walls were covered with oil paintings of gloomy-faced ancestors, along with countless antiques, guns, swords, and shields, not a spot of rust on any of them. Isabella wondered who was tasked with cleaning them. Her dreamy thoughts were interrupted by the sound of shouting coming from the hallway.

Probably one of the rich people getting frustrated at having to play the servant, she thought, rolling her eyes.

To her shock and horror, her father burst through the double doors. The man who had been opening the doors stumbled after him, trying to hold him back. The room fell silent, and all eyes were on him; the only sound was his angry, heavy breaths. He scanned the faces of the servants, and then the people in finery, seated at the table. She was frozen in terror as his gaze fell upon her.

"Isabella!" he cried out.

Everyone looked from him to her.

"I am here to bring you home."

Her mouth dropped open.

"It seems like the rumors I've heard are true," he continued, shaking his head. "I found all those filthy books you had, stuffed under your bed. So, I can guess at what kind of things you've done to be sitting at the top of a table, in a grand house. There is no way that this young man has married you, and I don't want to know how you have disgraced yourself. If you are very lucky, the poor young man that you abandoned might still be willing to marry you. You will have to be very apologetic, and finally, learn to behave yourself."

She didn't know what emotion to feel first. She flushed with shame, all the attention she was getting, and not the kind she was imagining that she would get at her festival.

Everyone knows, she thought. *They all know that I'm a runaway, that I was meant to be married off.*

Her father had broken free of the man's grasp and was storming alongside the table, up toward Isabella. Her heart was pounding as she feared whatever he was going to do. Garrett and Catherine flung back their chairs and stood up as if they hoped to protect her from him. She shut her eyes, wishing that she could just disappear, open up the black and white tiled floor and slide down into the kitchens below. If she hadn't mentioned the Festival of the Wheel of Fortune, she wouldn't have been out in the open like this, and he wouldn't have been able to find her.

She heard a clatter of metal as trays of food hit the tiled floor. She opened one eye.

Her father had barged past the people that he had believed to be servants. He stood over her.

"Get up and get out of those tart's rags, you're coming home."

"That is an interesting idea of home you have." The Mistress laughed from behind him.

He wheeled around to see her, dressed in a servant's uniform, pulling a slim sword from a bracket on the wall.

"Surely 'home' would be a place where a girl feels cherished, respected, and loved?" she said, brandishing the sword with a dark and mischievous look in her eye. "Are you cherishing your daughter by speaking to her like that? By threatening to marry her off?"

It was Isabella's father's turn to stand and stare in shock. Her Mistress shook her hair out of its restricting bun, letting it fall in flaming curls around her shoulders. She pointed the tip of the sword toward him. Isabella felt a shiver move down her spine as she saw the corner of her Mistress' mouth turn up.

"What would you know about any of this? Who are you?" Isabella's father spat.

"I am Elizabeth Mordancross and this is my house," she said. "I know Isabella far better than you ever will. She is not what you say she is, and she will not be going with you. She is going to stay here, with me. And no man of your choosing is going to be allowed to glance in her direction!"

Chapter 13

It was difficult to sit down and try to eat after all the drama they had just witnessed. Isabella picked at a piece of bread in silence. She kept her head down and avoided the glances of the others at the table. Garrett and Elizabeth escorted her father outside, barring the gates behind him.

"He's gone now," Catherine assured Isabella, patting her on the arm.

"I know," she sighed, worried that the others in the room were trying to hear what she was saying. "I had just left that old life behind and I didn't want to think about it. Now everyone knows where I come from. I wanted to keep that a secret."

"Look, people may talk, everyone loves a bit of gossip, they'll be interested in knowing about the man that you didn't want to marry, but no one is going to judge you."

Isabella gave a weak smile. "I'm glad you think so."

Her fun ruined, Isabella retreated to the bedroom that the Mistress had dressed her in that morning. Isabella sat on a wide stool in front of the mirror, feeling defeated. She took the necklace off, feeling as if the finery didn't suit her anymore. There was a gentle knock at the door.

"Who is it?" Isabella called, wishing she could get a moment by herself to process her feelings.

The Mistress stepped in, looking dishevelled from her sword-wielding. Her eyes were wide and full of tears.

"My sweet girl," she murmured, closing the door, and coming to stand behind Isabella. "Are you feeling al right?"

Isabella sniffed. "You were there, you heard what he said."

Elizabeth put her arms around her, "I heard what he said, and I think he is pathetic. I protected you because you deserve to be free from him."

"What if he comes back?"

"That is something we have to prepare for. I can throw him off my property, but as you are his daughter, he does have a claim to you, and he could come back, with solicitors and policemen."

"Could you help me get out of this?" Isabella asked, gesturing to the red silk dress.

"Of course. I want you to know that I won't let him take you away easily. I won't let him marry you off to…to…what was his name?"

"Phillip," Isabella said, tasting venom as she said it.

"Phillip, ugh. I am imagining that he is incredibly dull and unattractive, and not like me at all."

Isabella laughed. "He is absolutely nothing like you!"

"I am so happy to see you smiling again," Elizabeth said, getting the last of the buttons of the dress undone.

"I can't imagine Phillip with a sword. You looked

amazing by the way. It was very distracting, with my father being a party ruiner, but you looked like some kind of Irish warrior queen."

"Maybe that's what I was in a previous life," she said, straightening up again, "and you could have been my bodyguard, stoic and beautiful."

"That doesn't sound much like me."

"The beautiful part does."

She silenced Isabella's futile protests with a kiss. The red silk dress fell to the floor. The Mistress opened one eye to watch them in the mirror. She had one hand on Isabella's chin, tilting her face up to meet her. Isabella's chemise drooped off the shoulders, showing her delicate collarbones.

"We will do anything you like, tonight," the Mistress breathed. "I am still your servant."

Isabella let out a little gasp. "I know what I want, something that you've never done for me, but please, just let me kiss you for a while first."

Isabella sat down on the stool and saw herself, reflected in the mirror by the bed. She had her Mistress standing between her legs. She looked up into Elizabeth's eyes.

"My life is so crazy, Elizabeth!"

Her Mistress smiled. "But so good!"

Elizabeth bent down and kissed Isabella's forehead. She tilted Isabella's face up with one hand. Isabella felt all her worries melt away with the softness of her lips. She touched her tongue against Elizabeth's lower lip, and she opened her mouth. Isabella could feel that she was smiling.

"On your knees," Isabella murmured sweetly.

She was already breathing heavily as Elizabeth

unbuttoned her drawers. The restrictive corset stopped her from taking full deep breaths.

"I don't imagine you giving a lot of lip service," Isabella whispered.

"That's where you are wrong. There were many women, back in my wilder days. I am going to make you cum so many times, tonight."

Elizabeth hooked her arms around Isabella's thighs and pulled her toward her, letting her back rest on the wide plush stool. Her quick tongue circled the soft skin on Isabella's inner thigh, grazing it with her teeth and making her shiver. She moved upward, along her smooth inner thigh. She sank her teeth into her thigh, drawing a small cry from her. Isabella wanted her to bite her again, and she buried her hands in Elizabeth's thick hair. She bit her again, her perfect white teeth sharp, and she cried out. The Mistress moved her mouth to the velvet between Isabella's legs.

She tasted her opening, wet and wanting, then up, placing her full lips on Isabella's clit. She took her mouth away and licked her lips, running her pointed tongue over them. Her warm and wet lips touched Isabella again, softly, teasing her. Isabella grabbed a handful of Elizabeth's hair. Elizabeth's tongue urged Isabella's clit into Elizabeth's mouth. Isabella stretched out her legs as she relished in the sensation of this woman, her Mistress, on her knees, serving her with her perfect mouth. Her hot breath, and her warm mouth making her breaths quicker.

She wondered what stories Elizabeth had about doing

this, and she wondered if this was an experience that she would find worth writing about. She hoped it would be.

She held Isabella's thigh with one hand, and the other snaked between her legs. She spread her legs wider. Elizabeth parted the lips with two fingers, feeling the mixture of saliva and Isabella's wetness, preparing her to be entered and pleasured. She moved her index finger into her. Isabella gasped. She opened her eyes and watched herself, lying back on the cushioned stool, her pale legs over the Mistress's shoulders, still dressed in her maid outfit, her head between Isabella's legs. Her mouth was experienced; Isabella could tell, in the way that her lips caressed and sucked, her tongue relentless.

Elizabeth moved her second finger in, slow and teasing, getting Isabella to grind her hips into her hand, getting her to fill her. Isabella could hardly breathe, her Mistress was going to make her cum. She felt as if she was going to explode as she moaned and rithed.

Elizabeth smiled up at her, wiping the wetness off her face.

"We aren't done," Isabella whispered breathlessly.

The room was well equipped, and Isabella enjoyed having the Mistress watch her as she picked out what to use. Isabella wound a silk rope between her hands. Elizabeth unlaced Isabella's corset, and she took her chemise off, leaving her completely nude.

"Now, you undress for me, Elizabeth, I need you to take everything off."

Elizabeth was confident and curious, interested in whatever plans Isabella had for her. Isabella could understand the appeal of the uniform, its plain colors meant that it did not distract away from the beauty of the woman wearing it. Apron off, exposing the fine dressmaking that fitted her perfectly. She undid the buttons, exposing her lacy undergarments. Isabella slipped her hand between her legs and started to circle her clit, unsure whether she would be able to last to do what she wanted to do.

Elizabeth stood naked in front of her, the mass of red curls cascading down over her full chest. Isabella took in every inch of her.

"Bring the stool into the middle of the floor," Isabella said.

Elizabeth sat on the stool as Isabella blindfolded her, making a tight knot at the back of her head. The stool was wide enough that both of them could have sat on it together. She moved her into a lying position, her arms hanging at the sides, and her feet touching the floor. Isabella felt the silk rope between her hands. For once, it wasn't going to be used on her. She watched Elizabeth's face as she tied her wrists to the legs of the stool. She watched her mouth open, and a smile formed on her lips. She tied her ankles tight to the legs of the stool and ran her hands up Elizabeth's restrained body. Her thighs, firm from all of her horse riding, the curve of her belly, her soft and full breasts. Isabella picked up a bottle of massage oil and uncorked it. Elizabeth jerked about as Isabella poured a measure out across her chest, flinching from the cold liquid. Isabella kneeled next to her and worked the oil into her skin. She loved the feel of Elizabeth's breasts in her hands, so smooth and slippery with the oil. Her nipples hardened under

Isabella's deft fingers, and her face, half-hidden with the blindfold, could not conceal her feelings. Isabella caught herself almost drooling at the sight of Elizabeth's slick body. Isabella unboxed one of the dildos. She saw goosebumps raise on Elizabeth's body as she recognised the familiar sound.

"Open wide for me," Isabella whispered, holding her Mistress by the chin, her fingers by the edge of her mouth.

Elizabeth obeyed and opened her mouth. Isabella felt herself tighten as she saw those plump lips around the dark dildo. She drew it out, slick with saliva, and plunged it in again; she didn't gag, an expert in taking such things.

Isabella took it out and kissed her. "You've got it all ready for yourself. Do you want it inside you?"

"Yes!"

"Yes, what?"

"Yes, please, my goddess."

Isabella smiled, and she felt herself clench. She was so turned on that she could barely stand it, but she knew that it was going to be worth the wait.

The Mistress arched her back as Isabella pressed the end of the dildo to her opening, slick and warm with her drool. She repositioned herself, allowing Isabella to slide it into her.

She let out a long moan as Isabella pressed it into her, clenching around it. Elizabeth continued to moan as Isabella stood up. She stepped around to Elizabeth's head and straddled her face. Isabella placed one hand on Elizabeth's shoulder, the other one on Elizabeth's clit. She settled onto her Mistress' face, and Elizabeth quickly found Isabella's clit, and took it into her mouth.

Isabella rubbed Elizabeth's clit with two fingers, her moans muffled by Isabella on top of her. Isabella watched herself in the mirror, seeing Elizabeth strain against the silk rope, the dildo deep inside her, as she flexed and tensed on it. Isabella saw herself, her thighs around Elizabeth's beautiful face, silencing her with her body, her wetness.

Isabella edged closer as Elizabeth worked at her with her tongue and her mouth. She felt so right like this, in control. The feeling of her exquisite Mistress, bound and underneath her. Isabella rocked her hips back and forth, and Elizabeth kept up, moving her mouth to join with her. Isabella cried out as she came; she had known that she wouldn't be able to last long. She clenched her thighs around Elizabeth's head, and she sucked hard, drawing every inch of pleasure out of Isabella, leaving her a shaking mess.

Isabella dismounted, almost unable to walk. She kneeled between Elizabeth's legs, still tied to the legs of the stool.

"If I were your Mistress, I would be merciful," Isabella whispered. "No one would leave me without their needs met."

She delighted in how wet the dildo was when she drew it out, her Mistress shuddering with pleasure as she did. Isabella licked it, loving the taste of her Mistress. Isabella kneeled up, with the dildo between her legs, and she squatted down onto it, covering it in her cum.

She took it out again and leaned over Elizabeth.

"Open up, I want you to taste both of us, together."

Elizabeth moaned as the dildo, wet with herself and Isabella, slid into her mouth.

"Do we taste wonderful together?"

She spread Elizabeth's legs again and kneeled between them. All the teasing had left her so wet. Isabella played with Elizabeth's clit as she slid the dildo in, watching the expressions on her blindfolded face. She was leaning her head back, her mouth open.

There was a knock at the door.

"Give me a second!" Isabella called, hastily throwing a robe on. She left her Mistress with the dildo deep inside.

She opened the door, creating a narrow gap where only her face could be seen. It was the master at the door, still dressed in his servant's uniform.

"Master Garrett sent me to see how you are feeling. There is music and dancing downstairs, and everyone would like it if you joined in."

"Perhaps in a while." Then she had an idea. "Perhaps you could come in for a minute or two."

He stepped in, and she turned the key in the lock, closing them in. He gasped when he saw the situation his beautiful wife was in.

"Would you care to join us?" Isabella asked, mischief in her voice, looking up at him from under her eyelashes.

He nodded, soundlessly. She unbuttoned his trousers; he was wearing nothing underneath.

"Open wide, Elizabeth, you need to get it all wet for me," Isabella whispered, holding her Mistress' chin.

Isabella guided Thomas' cock into Elizabeth's mouth;

her tongue was eager. He let out a cry as she took it deep into her throat.

Isabella got back between Elizabeth's legs, this time on all fours.

"Thomas," Isabella whispered, "I want you to fuck me."

She heard him move around behind her and felt his his hands on her hips. Isabella started to fuck her Mistress with the dildo. Isabella gasped as the master teased her with the end of his cock.

"How do you want me?" he whispered.

"As slow as you can," she whispered back.

He took his time entering her, she leaned her head back as he moved into her.

"Just like that," she murmured, as he moved his cock slowly in and out of her, allowing her to savor every inch of his throbbing cock.

Isabella buried her face in her Mistress, taking in her sweet smell and taste. She loved the feeling of the bound woman struggling under her, writhing with all of the sensations Isabella was creating for her. The long, curved dildo reached inside Elizabeth.

Isabella had never felt anything like it, the way the master gripped her hips, the feel of each of his fingers pressing into her hips, the grind of him against her from behind. She heard Elizabeth's moans getting louder. The master started to play with Isabella's clit, reaching between her legs. Isabella worked the dildo faster and faster, and she felt herself getting close to cumming again. The master responded to her movements and pushed deeper and harder into her.

Elizabeth threw her head back and arched her back, and Isabella grabbed her by the hips, pulling her as close as she could and made her cum. She took the dildo out and tasted Elizabeth, licking and kissing her wetness, open-mouthed and tonguing her, overwhelming her and Isabella herself, as she was fucked harder and harder.

Isabella stopped him; she had another decadent idea. She lay down on top of Elizabeth, face to face and chest to chest. She kissed her eager mouth, excited for what was to come.

The master held his cock in one hand and entered Elizabeth, who arched her back, pushing against Isabella, who kissed her neck. She was still sensitive from orgasming. He slammed into her, rocking the stool under them. After a few thrusts, he switched into Isabella and held her hips as he fucked her on top of his wife. Isabella could feel Elizabeth's sweet, round breasts, the hair between her legs, all pressed up against her. She couldn't focus. He took his cock out of her and started to fuck the bound Elizabeth again. Isabella drank in her hot moans; she was excited and overwhelmed, mentally begging to get filled up again.

As if he had read her mind, he moved back into her. All their liquids mingled, and Isabella found herself drooling onto Elizabeth's beautiful and blindfolded face. Isabella wished for a second that she could be him, and have two delicious women waiting to be ravaged, wet and begging. He plunged into her again, and she realised that she was happy to be in this position. Her eyes rolled back as she felt Elizabeth's breasts jiggle underneath her.

He pulled out of her and thrust hard into his wife.

"Aw," the master teased. "Disappointed, Miss Isabella? Do you want to come?"

Isabella moaned in response, burying her face in Elizabeth's neck as he entered her again. His hips smacking into the round of her buttocks, filling her with all of his length.

Her lips found Elizabeth's as she came, her hips hard against her. She cried out, and Elizabeth smiled.

Elizabeth and Isabella sat on the bed together, legs intertwined. There were red marks on Elizabeth's wrists and ankles from where she had strained against the ropes. The master sat on the stool, his cock in his hand.

"It seems that Miss Isabella still wants you to come," Elizabeth said, brushing a lock of hair out of Isabella's face. "So, entertain the sweet girl."

Isabella watched his hand move up and down the length of his cock. Its tip was dark and wet.

"It made you so hard, didn't it?" Isabella asked. "Getting to be in both of us."

"It did, Miss Isabella," he replied, breathing harder.

"And you know how blessed you are? How many other men and women would love to be in your position?"

"Yes!" he cried out. "I know, I know how lucky I am!"

"And you want to make me happy, don't you?"

"Oh, more than anything, Miss Isabella!"

"Then you should come for me, cover your hands in your sweet, hot, cum."

He cried out, throwing his head back, as he cupped his

hands around his cock. He dipped his head, hair hiding his face. Isabella unwrapped herself from Elizabeth and walked toward him. Isabella pulled an embroidered handkerchief from his pocket and wrapped it around his cock, absorbing his lust.

Chapter 14

Elizabeth redressed Isabella into a fine satin dress. She couldn't believe how much fabric was built up into the dress. The bustle stuck out behind her, ruffles, and pleats covered the length of it.

"Your party dress, Isabella," Elizabeth murmured. "I had to make you presentable after all that we had been up to."

Isabella had a bit of difficulty recognising herself in the mirror, Elizabeth had worked magic on her.

Downstairs, everyone seemed to have forgotten about the drama from earlier, which was a relief for Isabella. She was more than happy to try to put it behind her. She was sure that her father had reached home, and was huffing and puffing at her speechless mother. Isabella shook her head, trying to get rid of the image of them, red-faced by the smoky hearth.

Garrett and Catherine looked thrilled to see her.

"I thought that you wouldn't come back down," Catherine said, grabbing Isabella's hand.

"Oh, I wouldn't be shaken for long," Isabella said, forcing a wide smile.

A string band was playing dance tunes, and everyone seemed to have made avail of the free drinks. Isabella downed a glass of white wine to catch up. She caught some glimpses her way, eyes scanning her face for signs of upset. She ignored them, holding her head up high, shaking her long curls around her shoulders.

"Do you want to dance, Catherine?" Isabella asked, making her flush.

"Of course, but wouldn't everyone look at us?"

"Look at them." Isabella smirked, glancing toward her drunk co-workers. "I'm sure they wouldn't mind if two friends wanted to dance."

Isabella took her hand and helped her up.

"I haven't danced at all tonight." Catherine sighed.

"And why was that?"

"Well, I was worried about you, and, you know, I am a bit easily embarrassed."

"You'll get over it in a minute."

Catherine glanced about herself, but no one was looking in her direction.

"I'm so glad you feel all right, Isabella. I was so scared for you."

Isabella said nothing and twirled her.

"But I hope you know that everyone is trying to get away from something. Maybe the stories aren't as dramatic as yours, but we are all escaping something."

"Are you?"

"Of course," Catherine said. "My mum was going to

have another baby, and she wanted me to care for the little one, and I knew that I wouldn't be able to stand it. I send some money home to help, but I'm not cut out for wrangling with a screaming baby."

"Then we understand each other?"

"Everyone understands you. Too many people marry without love, and they are miserable. You don't owe it to your parents to be another woman in a loveless marriage. We should all aim to find someone who is proud of us, and inspires us."

Isabella could tell that Catherine had had a few drinks herself. Their hands were sweaty, clasped together, and their dance had been little more than stepping in a circle, and a few twirls.

"And what are you looking for, Catherine?" "My muse, of course." She laughed.

"Did I not do a good job of that last night?"

"You did, I had never got to do anything like that before. It made me feel like I was at some sort of fancy art college, like in London or Paris."

"'t felt a bit scandalous, didn't it?" Isabella said, smiling.

"It did, it was exciting, I can see why you like her," Catherine said, stealing a glance over at the Mistress.

Elizabeth was dressed again into her uniform and was talking to a tall woman, dressed similarly.

"I'll never forget her with the sword," Isabella said, giving Catherine another twirl.

"I wish I could have done that. I wanted to protect you from him, but I didn't know what to do."

Catherine was out of breath and wanted to sit down.

She seemed to prefer to watch everyone anyway. Garrett extended a hand to Isabella when he saw her looking impatient.

"Would the lady of the house care to dance?"

"I am only the lady of the house for tonight."

"Oh, well, that's good enough."

He had discarded the cravat, so he looked more like himself, and he had let his hair down so that it curled down his neck.

"Let's pretend that earlier never happened," she said, as she saw him open his mouth.

"I want to be distracted for a while."

"Understandable."

"But aren't you sad that you aren't the only person who knows my secret now?"

"I thought you just said you didn't want to talk about it. Perhaps I am a little bit, but I do still have something on you."

"And what is that?"

"That you've kissed me."

She gave him a withering look, and he pulled her in close. She could feel the thud of his heart and his hands tightened around hers.

It was two in the morning before she considered going to bed. Once she left the ballroom, it felt as if everyone who had been in there were following her.

"I will escort you to your room, my lady." The Mistress smiled, a conspiratorial look in her eye.

Isabella laughed her off, but as she got closer to the bedroom, she figured out what was happening. Garrett was outside the room, a blush glinting across the tops of his cheeks.

The maids and kitchen staff huddled around giggling.

"Are the master and Mistress ready to be prepared for bed?" the real master enquired.

Isabella's mouth dropped open; she had not realised that this was going to be part of it.

The master and Mistress, dressed in their servants' clothes, escorted Isabella and Garrett in.

"Aren't you going to…close the door," Garrett said, gesturing to the doorway, where it seemed that the entire staff was gathering.

"No, I think we should leave it open," the Mistress said.

Isabella and Garrett faced each other. The master was behind Garrett, and the Mistress behind her, her hands on Isabella's shoulders. All her touches felt like so much more when there was an audience. As if everyone could imagine the Mistress' fingers on her naked skin.

Isabella kept her eyes on Garrett's face, which had turned bright red.

The Mistress started to unbutton Isabella's dress at the back, feeling her fingers tiptoe along her spine. The master removed Garrett's tailcoat. The collar of his shirt had collapsed when he took his cravat off. There were excited whispers from the doorway. Isabella wondered which of them they were more excited to see. Soon the Mistress had Isabella's dress over her arm, leaving Isabella in her corset, chemise and petticoats. Garrett looked uncomfortable; the wine seemed to have not helped to steady his nerves. Isabella tried not to let her eyes wander too much; she could tell that he had an athletic physique. The ladies in the doorway whistled and stamped their feet, as they took in Isabella in her petticoats and Garrett's firm thighs in tight trousers. A hint of purple embarrassment crept in Garrett's face as the master unbuttoned his shirt from behind, his long fingers exposing extra inches of weather tanned skin.

The master waited for them to catch up, leaving Garrett's trousers on. Isabella's corset was unclasped, and she felt her body relax, and her breasts move back into a more natural position. She was sure that the hardness of her nipples could be seen through the almost sheer fabric. Her petticoats covered the floor around her.

She was wearing only a fine chemise, her stockings and shoes, and Garrett was wearing only dark trousers, having stepped out of his boots. Isabella felt her face reddening as the Mistress grasped the bottom of her chemise, her warm fingers grazed Isabella's calves.

In a swift movement, she pulled the chemise over Isabella's head, exposing her naked body. Her co-workers screamed and clapped from the doorway. Garrett kept his eyes firmly on Isabella's face. The master unbuttoned Garrett's trousers, then pulled them down around his ankles, showing that he was wearing nothing underneath.

"Better leave the happy couple alone together," said the master with a laugh, scooping up the clothes he had taken from Garrett. There were groans of disappointment as the door clicked shut behind the Mistress.

Isabella crossed her hands over her chest. Garrett lowered his hands to conceal his hardening.

"This is something else." Garrett laughed, trying to fill the silence.

Isabella turned away to search in the drawers. "There must be something here that I can wear!"

The room had been cleared out before their arrival. Garrett averted his eyes as she bent over to search. She couldn't find anything. She slipped into the bed and held the sheet around her chest to conceal herself.

"So where am I meant to sleep?" Garrett asked.

Isabella looked at him. Light freckles trailed from his face down onto his chest. His cheeks were red from the wine. She could tell that he was embarrassed. She admired the curve of his biceps, his arms across his stomach, in a vain attempt to cover himself up.

"Well, you can sleep here."

He got into the bed, concealed his lower half with the blanket. Up close, she could see the dark hairs that led from his stomach down, and she could see the firmness of his chest.

Why am I so awkward with him? she wondered. *The master and Mistress act as if everything we do is normal, but I know that most people would not see it that way.*

"Not going to say anything?" Garrett asked.

"What am I supposed to say?"

"Did you know that this would happen when you were planning your festival?"

Isabella snorted. "Of course not! You don't honestly

think I suggested this in the hope of getting into bed with you?"

"I guess I never know what it is that you think, Miss Isabella."

"And that's the way that I want it to be. It keeps everyone on their toes."

"Can I tell you about what I want?"

"What is it?"

"I'd like you to kiss me again."

Isabella laughed. She couldn't help feeling flattered.

"Wasn't that a lifetime ago, Garrett?" She leaned up on her elbow.

"Only a matter of weeks." He sighed. "As if I could ever forget it. Hell, blame the drink. I had told myself never to tell you. I knew I could never compete because I have seen the way that she looks at you."

"Who?"

"Mistress Elizabeth. I've seen her eyes all over you. How could I be anything next to her?"

"How could any of us?" Isabella laughed.

"Has she…prepositioned you?"

Isabella took a second before answering. "Yes, she has."

"She kissed me, in the stables once, and she asked if I wanted to do more, and I wanted to, but I was too scared."

Isabella felt a twinge of jealousy, but of who she was jealous of, not too sure. Her Mistress could never be hers, not entirely; she was a married woman.

"I have said yes to her," Isabella whispered. "And I have enjoyed it, so, so much."

Garrett stared at her, taking it in. Isabella could not

believe that she had told him, but what did it matter anymore?

"Are you judging me?" she asked.

"No." He sighed. "I'm just trying to figure you out? Are you only inclined toward women?"

Isabella smiled. "No, I see the appeals of men as well, but I could never be subservient to one."

Garrett laughed. "And so you shouldn't be."

"Do you still want that kiss?"

"Of course."

He felt shy and careful. His mouth was closed when her lips met his. She could smell the expensive wine on him. She parted her lips, and he followed. His hands crept up to her face, and he touched the line of her jaw. She leaned into him, greedily, pressing her lips hard against his. Garrett pulled back, flushing, the redness spreading from his cheeks down onto his neck.

"What are you thinking about, Garrett?" she asked, tasting his name.

"I was imagining you as my wife, Isabella." he said, meeting her eye.

"Your wife?" She laughed. He sounded so formal and careful.

She stopped her giggle when she saw the serious look on his handsome face.

"I'm serious, Isabella, we could have a nice house, and a warm bed, together."

"But you know that I would not be a good wife?"

"I know that, but I could be good enough for the two of us." He smiled then. "Oh,

God, you must think that I am so ridiculous."

"I always liked you, Garrett."

"Is this how you turn me down nicely?"

"I saw you a lot, back in the village. You know that there were few people our age there. You never went to church, because if you did, I surely would have seen you there. I did all the shopping for my parents, oh and I sneaked away to chat with pedlars, hoping that they had something racy for me. Sometimes, when I was weighed down with a basket of vegetables, I would glance at you, at the stables by the traveller's inn."

"The day you kissed me was not the first time I saw you." He smiled. "I had a lot of time to watch people, and I loved to see you. I always wished that you would want to travel somewhere, to give me the chance to talk to you."

"So, is this me kindly turning you down? No, I do not need to be false with you. I am happy with my situation, and I do not need a husband. What would I do with one?"

He had looked down as if he was focusing on a loose thread on the luxurious bed sheets. "That's exactly the sort of thing that I expected you to say. That is who you are. In fact, I might have been a bit disappointed if you had been waiting for me to ask."

Isabella laughed. "I am not waiting around for anyone!"

"Apart from her."

"Yes, apart from her."

Chapter 15

Isabella had never slept in anyone's arms before. They had kissed again. She had leaned in first, his eyes reflected golden in the low lamplight before he closed his eyes. She touched his bare shoulders, taking in his soft skin, the rise of his collarbones. She got to take her time, brushing his hair behind his ear. She fell asleep with her head on his shoulder, feeling the pounding of his heart, his hand resting on her arm.

Isabella woke up to a knock at the door.

"Who is it?" she called, untangling herself from Garrett's warm arms. Her mouth and lips were dry.

"It's Catherine, I have something for you to wear."

Isabella smiled to see her friend, as she peeked out from behind the heavy door, then she was disappointed to see the maid's uniform that Catherine carried.

"How was it?" Catherine whispered, hearing Garrett's soft snores. "Did you..."

"No." Isabella shook her head. "No! Sure, we were exhausted, and drunk and..."

Catherine gave a wry smile, "...you can do better anyway."

"Oh?"

"But I'm sure that you knew that already."

"Why?" Isabella asked, glancing back at Garrett's sleeping form, his mouth hanging open. "What do you think is wrong with him?"

"Well, he's a man, isn't he?" Catherine winked, pulling the door shut behind her.

Isabella laid out Garrett's clothes at the end of the bed. She sighed. It felt like a brutal comedown. She dressed back into the maid uniform. The image of her Mistress dressed the same way lingered in her mind. A scarlet curl escaping from her high bun and tickling her nose. Isabella sighed again. She had been so lucky, if only it could have lasted longer.

Garrett stirred as she tied her apron on, "You're up already?"

"Back to normal life, Garrett."

"Well, as normal as life gets, for a concubine pretending to be a maid." He had a mischievous grin, and it suited him.

"If you had any sense, you would be a concubine pretending to be a groom."

He laughed, throwing the sheets back, and swinging his legs out of bed. In the daylight, she could see that it was only his face and forearms that were tanned and freckled. She had heard that 'was called a farmer's tan. His legs and buttocks were as good as she had hoped that they would be; all the horse riding that he did showed. He pulled a loose, white shirt on, leaving it open. She stole a look down, and saw his cock, hard, curving up to touch his firm stomach. He turned away from her, pulling his tight trousers on. She thought that he must be doing it on purpose when he had to wriggle a bit to get the inflexible fabric up over his round buttocks. One hand glided over his bottom, to smooth out the fabric. She held a gasp in, she should have known that he never wore any underwear. He ran his fingers through his wavy hair and tied it back with a string from around his wrist.

He glanced over his shoulder at her. "You know where to find me."

She nodded. "That was a wonderful day that we had, wasn't it?"

He agreed and kissed her on the cheek. "I will see you around, Isabella."

She sat down on the end of the bed, still exhausted. Her stomach gave a tell-tale rumble, and she reluctantly pulled her shoes on.

When she was at the top of the stairs, she saw the Mistress standing by the front door with the tall, slightly older woman that she had seen her with the previous night. The other woman had a foreign accent, and an elegance that made Isabella think that she was French. The French woman was leaning down, a smile on her face, and the pretty Mistress was whispering in her ear. The Mistress was dressed normally again, in a bustle dress of dark linen, taking Isabella's breath away.

This woman must be close with Elizabeth, Isabella thought.

Both glanced up when they heard Isabella's footsteps on the stairs. The Mistress beckoned her over.

"Oh, Isabella, you have to meet Aurelie. She is one of my oldest friends."

Aurelie took Isabella's hand and kissed it. "Elizabeth has told me much about you.

She made such a beauty of you last night, and today I can see your natural beauty."

"Oh, thank you." Isabella flushed, unsure of how nice she could look in her hungover state.

"Has Elizabeth told you about me?" Aurelie asked.

"I don't believe so," Isabella replied.

Aurelie looked at Elizabeth. "Oh, Elizabeth, after I taught you everything that you know?"

To Isabella's surprise, she saw her Mistress blush.

Aurelie smirked. "I will make sure that she tells you about some of our adventures."

The two women went back to whispering together, and Isabella went to get something to eat.

Isabella was not the only person looking a little worse for wear from the previous day. When she entered the staff dining room, she heard murmurs and whispers, speculating on her decadent night with Garrett. She didn't mind that much, knowing that many of them must have been jealous of her. Catherine was eating porridge, and Isabella did the same. She was hungry, but she knew that she was not going to be able to eat anything too heavy. Isabella was glad to hear the buzz in the room, to know that everyone had enjoyed the festival that was her idea. No one seemed to be mentioning the drama that there had been with her father.

She was happy to hear that people were discussing her and Garrett instead.

"I don't think that any work will be done today," Catherine said. "Everyone is so tired from yesterday." She had her sketch pad with her, and she was doodling circles.

"I'm sure the master and Mistress won't mind if we don't do anything today. What are you planning to do?" Isabella asked.

"We could finish that drawing if you would be interested?"

Isabella took some time in the bathroom getting clean and ready, cleaning away all hints of the excesses of the previous day. Catherine was already sitting on her bed, she had stripped down to her chemise, with her corset loosened for extra comfort and flexibility.

"I thought that being a bit undressed would help you feel more relaxed," Catherine said, seeming flustered.

For Catherine, this was harder than drawing Isabella in a room full of people. She tried to help Isabella get back into the position she had been in before, trying not to let her fingers linger on her cool, porcelain skin.

I have to feel like the artist, she told herself, as she set her art pad up. *I am the artist, not some silly girl.*

Catherine had to look at Isabella's naked form and recreate it on the page through pencil and charcoal. She had already started the outline two nights before. She worked on her face and her arms, feeling no shame or awkwardness. Once she inched down from her collarbones, she felt the heat in her cheeks rising. Isabella noticed this, seeing Catherine bowing her head more in concentration.

"Are you all right?" Isabella asked with a smirk.

"Of course!" Catherine said. "The experience is going to be so useful for me! When you see my pictures in art galleries up and down Europe, you will be able to credit yourself with helping me to get started."

Isabella stretched out her stiffening legs, modelling was harder work than she had expected it to be, and drawing a picture took longer than she thought it would, not that she knew much about art. Her mind wandered to some of the erotic illustrations that she had bought; they were just prints, cheap and crude. Catherine was creating something much better, and she was deep in concentration. Isabella closed her eyes, listening to the scratch of the pencil on the page, the birds singing outside on the lawns and her slow breaths.

Isabella must have fallen asleep because she woke up to Catherine whispering her name.

"I was just resting my eyes," Isabella said.

"Of course, you were." Catherine laughed. "I finished the picture."

Isabella opened her eyes. Catherine looked nervous; she was biting her lip and smiling. She turned the picture in her slim hands, letting her see it. Isabella swallowed; she loved it. Catherine had made her look lovely, her eyes wide, a knowing smile on her lips.

"Do you think the Mistress will like it?" Catherine asked.

"Are you planning to give it to her?"

"Yes, she is paying very generously for it. I hope that is all right with you?"

"Of course, I'm just flattered that she wants a picture of me."

"And do you like it?"

"Of course, you are amazing."

Catherine smiled widely. Isabella got up and pulled her chemise back on.

"Isabella?"

Isabella turned; Catherine kissed her on the lips breathlessly.

"I hope the Mistress was wrong." Catherine sighed. "I hope that you don't have to go away."

Chapter 16

Isabella held the drawing in both hands, her grip tightening as she thought about what Catherine had said.

What had she meant? Why did Elizabeth think that she wouldn't be able to stay?

She gritted her teeth; she wasn't going to let her family take her home.

There were elated voices on the other side of the library door. Isabella rapped the solid wood with her knuckles. The Mistress called for her to enter.

Elizabeth and Aurelie were curled up on the sofa together. The lights were low, and they looked up expectantly at the doorway as she entered.

"I was thinking about you." Aurelie smiled as Isabella stepped toward the pair.

"Catherine finished the drawing," Isabella said, handing it over.

The two women scanned the page, and then glanced over the top of it as if imagining her as she had looked that night.

Elizabeth set the picture on a side table.

"Sit with us," Aurelie said, shifting over, creating a space between herself and Elizabeth.

Isabella sat. Both the women had kicked their shoes off and had their legs folded onto the sofa, stocking covered toes touching Isabella's thighs. She could feel the heat radiating from them.

"Sweet Elizabeth wants to tell you about our adventures," Aurelie teased.

"Do I?" asked the Mistress, haughty and indignant.

"Of course, you do."

"Which one?"

"How about that night at the theatre?"

Elizabeth smiled, casting her eyes down. "I can do that."

"I will keep you right."

Elizabeth turned to Isabella...

Aurelie and I have been friends for quite a while. I went to France once I received my inheritance. I was in my early twenties, and more than ready to experience something outside of small English towns and country houses. Paris was a city of art and music, and I knew enough of the right people to get invited to the fashionable houses. However, I did not know anyone well enough to have friends, and my French was poor. I spent more evenings than I care to admit in the corner of some fine salon, eating biscuits, and admiring dresses, just to pass the time. I did not want to accept that I was not as sophisticated as these people.

One night, when I was three glasses of wine deep, Aurelie approached me. Even for a French woman, she was different.

She wore eye makeup and lipstick, which I had rarely seen outside of the theatre. She wore what looked like a military coat, finely tailored, over her bustled skirt.

"English girl?" she asked.

"Yes, how did you know?"

She shrugged. "Do you want to see the best sides of Paris?"

She took me to places that I never could have known about. Drinking clubs and dance shows, only attended by women. My eyes were opened. I had slept with someone once before, a convict, maybe I will tell you about that another time. But this was another level of decadence. My French improved so quickly. I had to learn so that I could get deeper into this beautiful world. Aurelie kissed me one night, and we ended up back at her apartment, but that is a different story.

Aurelie knew everyone, and could get tickets for anything, so she took me out all the time. People started to know my name and ask after me; she had made me seem exciting. Once, I was feeling homesick for dreary England, so she took me to see a play in English. It was a comedy about the gentry and their engagements. I cannot remember its title, but I do not recommend it.

Aurelie had booked us a box, of course, the best seats in the house, high up in this lovely theatre. We had to climb up many flights of stairs, and squeeze down corridors so narrow that our dresses would barely fit.

The air was hot that high up, we were fanning ourselves before the play had even started. The box next to us was empty, but I could see someone sitting in the box directly across from us. Aurelie was very proper and helped me into my seat. I had rather hoped that she would hold my hand during it, but even then, I knew she wasn't the type. Pretty quickly, we realised that the play was not going to be any good. The actors were wooden and the script was dull. I felt Aurelie's fingers on my cheek, cool from holding her glass, and it felt heavenly in that hot theatre. She leaned in to kiss me.

"In front of all these people, madame?" I asked.

"No one was looking up at us," she whispered back. "They are too taken with their stuffy, English play."

I smiled; she was the opposite of the uptight English. My aunts and cousins would not have survived meeting her, and God knows what they would have done, if they had seen me, kissing her at the theatre. Someone a bit more interesting did happen to see through.

Aurelie kissed me. I knew her lipstick would be all over my mouth, marking me out as her lover. The idea excited and scared me in almost equal measures.

"Are you glad I found you, ma choue anglaise?"

"Of course, I am."

"Uncross your legs."

My skirts shifted about as I removed one knee from the other, setting both feet on the floor, about shoulder-width apart. She gave me a flashing smile as she reached both hands down, pulling my layers of skirts up around my thighs. Over the front of the box, no one would be able to see, as it reached up to the height of my chest. I was wearing split drawers, so it was easy for her to reach my legs. Her cold hand trailed up my inner thigh.

"Here?" I whispered. "With all of these people?"

"Of course, my sweet."

She silenced me by running a finger between my lips, up to my clitoris. She settled two fingers on it and started to stroke. She started slowly and gently, putting on little pressure, teasing me with the prospect of more. I was grateful then for the rise of the orchestral music from below the stage. She leaned over me then, a smile forming as she reached the other hand between my spread legs. Her middle finger found my opening. She covered her finger in my wetness. She looked into my eyes, enjoying my reaction as I squirmed under her experienced touch.

I looked into her dark eyes, the flicker of the lamp lights reflecting in them, her slim smile making me want her more and more. She bit her lip. The edge of her sharp tongue moved over her lips and teeth. I was aware of everything, the plush velvet of the seat, and my fingers curled around the worked metal armrests as she got down on her knees in front of me.

Aurelie pushed my skirts further up, and I felt the beautiful cloth against my bare inner thighs.

Aurelie's warm mouth made contact with my skin, and she trailed her tongue up my leg. She placed her hands on my legs, edging them further apart. I felt exposed, with my skirts up around my waist in the crowded theatre. I could not hold back a gasp as she parted my lips with two fingers, feeling her manicured nails on my delicate skin. I trusted her; she knew what she was doing. My back was pressed hard against the chair. I kept my eyes ahead, trying to keep my mouth closed.

"Do not attract too much attention to yourself, my girl," Aurelie murmured.

"I will try not to," I whispered back, knowing that my breathless voice was lost under the roar of the chattering actors and orchestra.

With my lips spread, my clitoris stood out for her, and she worked her tongue up to it. I felt the hot spark, making its way up through me, catching in my chest and throat. The feel of her soft hair against my inner thigh. Her hot mouth around my clit. She started to suck, and I took a breath in, taking in the hot air, with all the mixture of smells, in. I could smell her perfume, knowing that she had sprayed it on her neck and behind her ears. Her slim neck, level with the seat of the chair. Her mouth was on me, and her full lips pressed against me.

She sucked, her tongue running up and flicking against my clit.

Her fingers moved back into me, so easily because of my arousal. I could feel her covered in my wetness, as she slid in and out of me. My eyes were caught by the golden decorations of the theatre as she fucked me, her first and middle fingers in me, up to the knuckles.

I knew that if I looked at her that I would come. The sight of her head bowed between my legs, as I gripped tighter and tighter around her. I could picture her fingers, drenched with my longing, as she pushed herself into me. Her plump lips around my swollen clit. She moved my hips, drawing me closer. I could feel her hot spit running down my inner thigh, and down onto the velvet seat. She gripped one of my legs, pulling me down in the chair. She tilted her head, showering my sensitive clit with kisses. She took it softly between her teeth, giving me gentle nips. It was taking all my strength not to cry out. Her hair was wound up in a thick plait, and I gripped it tightly with one hand. I heard her moan. The notion of her enjoying it was too much, and my eyes rolled back. I wanted her to enjoy me so much, the taste of me, the feel of me. I felt important and beautiful. She found me delicious, licking and sucking, entering, pushing herself inside me. Her elegant fingers were skillful, and she fingered me in a way that was far superior to anything that I had done myself. My hands worked through her hair, feeling her ears and her drop-down earrings. I touched her jaw, feeling the movement of her mouth, feeling her opening wider, and taking more of me in. I felt the rush and knew that I was close, pushing my hips up toward her, and she gripped my bottom, scrunching the cotton of my drawers against me. I tensed around her fingers, her grip on me. My head was forced back as I orgasmed for her, letting the feeling flow through me. When I looked down, I saw her smiling to herself, looking proud of what she had done to me. I was breathing hard, trying to steady myself; I could not believe what she had made me do.

"Aurelie," I sighed.

She got back up, slipping back into the seat by me. I could see the wetness around her mouth. She licked her lips and wiped it away on the back of her hand, leaving a smudge of dark lipstick. The play was ending, and across from us, in the box at the other end of the stage, I could see a man standing and clapping. His eyes were not on the bowing actors; they were on me.

"Who was he?" Isabella asked.

"The man that I would go on to marry." Elizabeth smiled, then continued…

A few minutes later, there was a knock on the door to our box, and a member of the theatre staff stood with a calling card on a silver dish. I tipped him and sat down by Aurelie.

"I think someone must have seen us," I said, my cheeks burning.

I read the card. It was written in poor French, "I saw you; you have hypnotised me."

It had his name and his rooms in Paris printed on it. He was still looking over at us.

"I do not particularly care for men." Aurelie smiled.

"I have been with one before," I said. "In an odd circumstance, it was almost as exciting as you."

The theatre lights came up, and I squinted in the brightness.

I ran into him in the foyer of the theatre. Aurelie held back as I spoke to him. He had the kind of narrow and fine features that I admire in a man. He seemed unsure of what to say.

"You are not French, are you?" I asked.

"Was my writing so poor that you could tell? No, disappointingly I am an Englishman. I hope you will forgive me."

"So how did you end up marrying Thomas?" Isabella asked. "Why didn't Aurelie come back here with you?"

Aurelie snorted.

"Aurelie was never the marrying type, and she certainly was not the type of person who would ever come and live in England."

"You do have a wonderful house, Elizabeth." Aurelie smiled. "But I could never live out here. For me, it's enough that you are happy to see me, and you share your bed with me."

"Aurelie still has her pick of the women in Paris," Elizabeth whispered.

Isabella could not help but feel curious about this French woman, and how different it would be to have sex with her. Isabella imagined her experience and her confidence. She caught herself glancing from Aurelie's lips, thinking about how her mouth must feel, then glancing downward to her long fingers, cupping a wine glass.

"So, Isabella, did you have your way with that young man last night?" Elizabeth asked, smiling up from under her lashes. "I think you have been wanting him for a while."

"No." Isabella shook her head. "We spoke instead."

"How odd," Aurelie said. "Two hot-blooded young people, naked under silk sheets.

That should have been a delightful recipe."

"Everything with him is a bit strange. We have a little bit of history together. He brought me here in the first place. He knew before anyone else that I was running away from my old life."

"Isabella desired me from first sight," Elizabeth said. "I suppose I felt the same way about her, even if she was in dowdy clothes, getting soaked in the rain."

Isabella smiled at the memory. "I thought that I was coming here to have a normal job, changing beds, not sharing them with you."

"But it is so much better this way," Elizabeth said.

Chapter 17

Isabella loved the summer weather, and she appreciated getting to do nothing. Hot weather used to mean frizzing hair and sweating over the stove. Instead, she was sitting on the lawn, feeling the sun on her skin. She held a cup and saucer. Isabella was up early, and so was Garrett. He had set up jumps for the horses, and he was leaping over them on the back of Bracken. His strong legs were clamped tightly around the horse. As he reached the jump, he leaned forward, rising from the saddle, and his hands moving up the horse's neck. He must have known that she was watching him, but he paid no attention. He never wore a hat when he was riding, and he did not dress like the grand lords when they were hunting. Instead of a tailored red coat and hat, he wore pale jodhpurs and a loose white shirt, the sleeves rolled up around his elbows. This was how she wanted to spend her mornings.

Garrett finished up and jumped down from the saddle easily.

"Hey!" Isabella called over to him, raising a hand.

Garrett gave a thin smile back and then hurried off, dragging the horse behind him, back to the stables. Isabella had taken a step forward and stopped, lowering her hand back to her side. She dusted herself off from sitting on the ground, hoping that Garrett was not feeling uncomfortable around her. It had been a relief for Isabella to speak candidly about what she had been doing at Mordancross House. Keeping secrets was tiring for her, and she had had enough of it.

Her Mistress asked for her in the afternoon and was told that she would find Isabella in the library. Isabella was stretched out on the sofa in the library, having discovered where Elizabeth kept her stash of erotic stories. They looked better than anything Isabella had owned. Instead of thin, stapled together pages, Elizabeth's collection consisted of real, bound books, with cloth covers. Elizabeth examined the title of the one that Isabella held.

"What do you think of it?" the Mistress asked.

"I'm enjoying how much detail there is, especially reading about how much fun the women are having. Many of the other books I have read have all been about the cock."

"And do you know why this writer is different?"

"Not really, there is no name on it."

"I wrote it."

"You didn't! How could you have?"

"It is only proper that I try to stay busy and have some of my own income. I also just enjoy daydreaming. I hope that I have taught you a thing or two about dreams or fantasies?"

"Of course, just like how Aurelie showed you."

"Oh Aurelie, she is on her way back to Paris today. Maybe in the winter, we could go to visit her. Have you ever been to France?"

"I have never left England."

"All the better, I cannot wait to show you."

"If I am still able to be here."

She watched Elizabeth's expression change, her smile fading away. "Why would you not be here, Isabella? You do not think that I am bored of you? I would never—"

"No, it wasn't that. All this with my father—"

"I can do what I can, Isabella, but I cannot make promises. I have offered him money, I have told him that you are safe and happy, but he does not care. He wants you married off. I am going to do my best, to keep you away from that life."

Isabella hugged Elizabeth tight. "Thank you, for everything."

When she looked into Elizabeth's eyes, she knew that she had caught her off guard.

"It is not a problem," Elizabeth murmured. "Besides, good things could still happen."

"What do you mean?"

"That is why I came to get you."

"What is it?"

"Come with me, we are going outside."

They exited through the back door, out into the yard. It seemed quiet compared to the last few days. Most of the shining carriages and glossy horses were gone, back away to wherever it was that the friends of the master and Mistress lived. The house had gone back to how it had been before.

Isabella followed her Mistress across the cobblestones, struggling to keep up with her long strides.

"Where are we going?' Isabella asked.

Elizabeth turned to face her, coils of red hair escaping from her elaborate coif. "Young Garrett is who we are going to see."

Elizabeth unlatched the door into the stables. The building was bright and clean. The horses shuffled in their stables. There was a freshly polished saddle on a stand. Elizbeth stood with one hand on her hip.

"Where is he?" she asked, glancing upward, then she called out his name.

There was a clatter on the stairs, and he appeared, a piece of straw in his hair. His eyes widened as he saw Isabella, and then forced a smile.

"What brings you ladies out to see me?"

"Come on down, Garrett," Elizabeth said.

He made his way down the creaking stairs, his eyes moving from Elizabeth to Isabella. He was trying to read their expressions.

"I wanted to ask about your night together," Elizabeth said, a light tone in her voice as if the topic meant nothing to her.

Garrett flushed and stuttered; Isabella froze.

"I have already asked Isabella about it," Elizabeth said.

"Well," Garrett started. "You were there for most of it—"

"Then continue from when I left the pair of you."

"We got into bed and we talked, she told me about you, and what you have done together."

Elizabeth smiled, and Isabella could tell that Elizabeth was loving the idea of them, naked in bed together, talking about the ways that Elizabeth had taken her.

"And did you have each other?" she asked.

Isabella could hear Garrett take a breath in, and he blushed. She waited to hear what he would say.

"We did not," he said after a pause.

"And did you want to?"

Garrett looked down at his feet, "Perhaps I did."

"And you, Isabella?"

She could not help but gasp, and she knew that she would not be able to lie to her Mistress. "I did want to."

Elizabeth smirked, her red lips parted, and her eyes closed. "The pair of you are so silly, are you not?"

Isabella and Garrett stared at the Mistress, and Isabella wished that he would say something to break the silence.

"You can make it up to me," Elizabeth said, a devious smile forming on her full lips.

Isabella glanced at Garrett and saw him swallow. Perhaps he was more intimidated by her than Isabella had thought.

"I have a little fun punishment. You like it when I punish you, don't you, Isabella?"

Isabella could feel Garrett's eyes on her, anticipating her response. "Well, I have enjoyed it before."

"Good," she smiled. "You will like this."

She clicked her fingers at Garrett and Isabella, and they followed her over to the saddle stand. Isabella had nervousness in her stomach. She was shocked that her Mistress would involve Garrett. Isabella had told him about her relationship with her Mistress. Now he was going to see what their relationship was like.

"Isabella." The Mistress sighed, reaching out her hands.

She took Isabella's wrists and leaned Isabella's forearms on the saddle. The Mistress pulled Isabella's skirt and petticoats up.

"But—but anyone could walk in!"

Elizabeth pushed her hips against Isabella, as she reached around and unbuttoned Isabella's drawers. She felt the cool of the buttons, and the warmth of her Mistress' skin as they pressed against her. Her skirts were piled up around her, so she could not look to see Garrett's expression.

"Now, Garrett, I am going to get you to do something that I know you are very good at."

She heard Garrett stutter, unable to take his blue eyes off Isabella, half-naked and bent over. The Mistress whispered something to him and gave him something. Isabella shifted to look back at them.

"No, Isabella, stay where you are," the Mistress said, walking around so that she could face her.

Elizabeth leaned over, pushing hair out of Isabella's face. "How are you always so pretty?"

There was a crack, and Isabella was stunned. A second later, she felt the sting across her bottom, and she realised what had happened. Garrett had whipped her. Once the pain hit her, she let out a frustrated cry.

"Oh God, Isabella, I am so sorry," Garrett murmured.

"Don't be sorry," the Mistress smiled. "Do it again."

Isabella tried to relax, knowing that it would only hurt

more if she tensed up. The whip whistled through the air and struck her again, leaving a bright red line across the cheeks.

She was breathing hard, and she had gripped the edge of the saddle stand.

"Up, now, Isabella," the Mistress said, extending a hand. "It's Garrett's turn now."

Isabella hastily pulled her drawers back up, and let her skirts tumble back down about her ankles. Garrett wore a stunned expression, and his body was turned as if he planned to run.

"Garrett," Elizabeth whispered. "Give Miss Isabella the whip."

Isabella took it, feeling its length and flexibility. The Mistress extended a hand to him, and Isabella could see that he was shaking. Now that it was over, Isabella did not see the issue. Yes, she had been a bit embarrassed, and it had hurt a bit, but she had enjoyed it.

Garrett and Mistress Elizabeth punishing her together was not a combination that she would have expected, but she wasn't complaining. Garrett, on the other hand, seemed mortified. Had Isabella's life got so strange that this was almost normal to her?

"Now, Isabella is going to whip you. How do you feel about that?"

Garrett looked up from his bent-over position. "Not the best, if I'm honest."

"And is that because of something that you have to tell her?"

"Yes, it is."

"Something you have to tell me?" Isabella asked. "Well, what is it?"

"You can wait a few minutes for that." Elizabeth smiled.

Garrett turned a bright red as the Mistress unbuttoned his jodhpurs. Isabella was enjoying the spectacle. It was a struggle for both of them because Garrett wore his trousers so tight around his firm thighs. Elizabeth could only get them down as far as his knees, on account of his long riding boots.

Isabella took a minute to take in what she was seeing. The pain of him whipping her was worth it for this. She placed the end of the whip at the small of his back, invoking a shiver from him. Isabella moved it down, and over his firm buttocks, making him twitch, then down over his thighs. She wanted to run her tongue up those strong thighs. She wanted to know how he felt, and know if this excited him.

Isabella struck him for the first time, and she heard a breath escape him. She watched as the redness developed on his skin. Elizabeth raised an eyebrow. Isabella found herself breathing hard. She ran one hand down the whip and tapped it against her hand.

Garrett laughed. "You are cruel, Isabella, building up suspense like this!"

He tensed up again as she raised the short whip again. It rushed through the air, and the second time, he let out a little moan. Isabella set the whip down, and Garrett gathered himself up, turning away from her as he pulled his trousers back up. His face was red, and he had difficulty meeting her eye.

"I feel much better now." Elizabeth smiled. "Now, Garrett, you have something to tell Isabella, don't you?"

"But I could wait?" he asked.

"No, you should tell her. Look at you, acting so awkward around her. She deserves to know why."

"Know what?" Isabella asked, starting to feel impatient.

"Please don't be angry at me," he sighed. "But I wrote to your father."

"My father?" Isabella said, almost choking.

"I wrote to him, asking him to forget about your fiancé."

"And why would he listen to you?" Isabella asked. "He won't listen to me, and I am his only child! He doesn't even know who you are!"

"I said he could forget about him, because there is someone else who wants to marry you, Isabella. It's me, I want to."

Isabella took a step back. "You did what?"

"I asked your father if I could marry you instead."

Chapter 18

Isabella's heart was pounding as she ran out of the stables, and out across the cobblestones, holding her skirts bunched in her hands. Once she reached the lawns, she slowed to a hasty walk, trying to catch her breath again.

What about what we talked about? she thought. *Did he listen to me at all? I said that that wasn't the life for me! Who does he think he is?*

She walked down the lanes toward the gates of the house. A clump of mushrooms had grown at the foot of one of the trees, and in her anger, she kicked them, scattering their parts over the manicured lawns. She shook her head, not believing what had happened.

Why would he do that? she asked. *Why would he write to him? My father doesn't own me.*

She sat down in the grass, facing the gate lodge of the house. She pushed her hair off her face.

Garrett, marrying me? she thought. *What has got into him?*

Then it dawned on her.

He thinks that I am going to be taken back as well. Even after everything that I said, he saw my father that night, saying that he wasn't going to give up. If I had to get married, marrying him would be better than ending up with Phillip. But that isn't what it should be about!

Isabella glanced up at the gate lodge. It was a sweet two-story building, with wooden eaves painted blue. She pictured what it was like inside, a cosy kitchen, with dark, wooden furniture. She imagined that the bedroom was upstairs, with a sloped ceiling, with the bed in the middle of the floor. If she lived there, she would have red bed sheets, and a huge wardrobe, full of beautiful clothes.

Imagine waking up in that sweet house, she thought. So cosy, and I would have my own space. Imagine waking up next to Garrett there.

She found herself blushing, finding herself silly for even thinking about it.

I'm not silly, she thought. *He was the one who asked to marry me.*

She imagined the warm bedroom, with the fire lit, and Garrett beside her, sleeping naked. She would wake him up, and he would kiss her, and she would enjoy the warmth of his arms. Because they would still be living at Mordancross House, Garrett would continue his work, training the horses.

She imagined stepping into the gate lodge, her house, and kicking her shoes off in the hall, Garrett would be in the kitchen, preparing dinner for both of them. He would be warm from his work and have a streak of dirt on his face. They would eat together and talk about their day. She dreamed that he would be a good cook, even though she had never heard him mention it. They would curl up on the sofa together and read. Everything that she would want from him, she knew that she could never get from Phillip. He would want her cooking, cleaning, and raising children, these things that she did not want to picture at all.

She thought about going to bed with Garrett every night and learning more and more about each other, and he would learn to understand her tastes. The Mistress would visit, and they would enjoy each other's company.

Fear struck Isabella. Maybe he wouldn't be all right with her continuing to see the Mistress. If Garrett was her husband, he would be able to stop her.

She heard someone pounding across the grass behind her, and she glanced around.

"Isabella!" Garrett called. His eyes were huge.

"What were you thinking?" she asked.

"I'm sorry, Isabella. I didn't ignore what you told me. I listened to everything that you said to me."

"It doesn't feel like it! And you knew yourself how I would react! That is why you were being so sneaky and secretive! Would you have told me if Elizabeth hadn't made you?

Or were you hoping my father would say yes, and then you would have sprung it on me?"

"I wasn't trying to spring anything on you!"

"Then what were you trying to do?"

"I don't know, I was impulsive, maybe I was wrong."

He came and sat down beside her. "Ouch," he winced. "I think that is still going to hurt for a while."

"You think that my father is going to come and get me, don't you?"

He nodded. "I'm worried about you."

She wanted to tell him not to worry, and that she could handle herself, but deep down, she knew the power her father had. Isabella knew that, legally, she was his property.

"So, is that why you wanted to marry me? Because you were worried about me?"

"I always knew you were running away, so it had to be bad. But it didn't feel quite real to me until that night, seeing him, how he spoke to you."

"Hmm, and not because you are madly in love with me?"

"Perhaps, when we get to know each other more. But seriously, I never meant to disrespect you, and anyway, we don't know what he is going to say."

"And what would life be like, Garrett, together?"

He stared at her and then smiled; she had caught him off guard. "Well, we could still live here, if you would like. Oh, I know! You could come and live in the stables with me!"

"Oh, goodness, no, that would be awful!"

"Would it be? I would make you breakfast every morning."

"Can you cook?"

"No, but I could learn…"

Isabella rolled her eyes dramatically at him, and then looked up at him. He was so earnest. There was something about his seriousness that made her want to laugh. "And would you be all right with what myself and the Mistress do?"

"Of course, I would allow it," he said.

"That's just it, you see?" Isabella said. "I don't want to have to be 'allowed'! It would not be fair and honest for me to marry anyone. I don't want to ask permission to live my life as I already have been."

"Even if your father says yes, we don't have to get married, we could live in sin. And I would never tell you what to do, your life should always belong to you. I'm trying to help you!"

They stared at each other in silence. Isabella didn't know what to say. He wasn't asking her to marry him to control her.

'Thank you, Garrett,' she sighed. 'I know that you were just trying to help me.'

Garrett walked Isabella back to the house, his arm holding hers. She felt as though she were in a daze. She had been unsure if Garrett even liked her, and now, he had asked to marry her.

She went looking for Catherine and found her making a bed on the first floor.

"Why are you all flushed?" Catherine asked.

"Am I?" Isabella asked, touching her face. "Garrett has written to my father, asking permission to marry me."

Catherine dropped the pillow she was holding, her mouth open, and she straightened her face. "How do you feel about that?"

"I'm not sure, that's why I wanted to speak to you about it."

"You know that I will be unhappy, no matter who you choose," Catherine said. "But I suppose Garrett is the better option. It seems that no matter what, you are going to be leaving here."

"Catherine, I don't want to get married! You must have noticed by now that I have too much to give just to be with one person. Marriage is not my goal, but I cannot risk my father marrying me off, that would be the end of everything."

Catherine sat on the bed. "I am sad for you. I'm so glad that my family have stopped trying to control my choices."

"I could run away again, I suppose."

"You got lucky once. There is no one else out there like our Mistress. I don't think that you could be that lucky a second time."

Isabella sat down as well. "Then what should I do?"

"Well." Catherine paused. "If you run away, don't do it alone."

Isabella looked into her eyes.

"I'll come with you," Catherine said, with a smile breaking out. "If you are going to leave, please tell me. Even if you end up somewhere horrible, at least we could be together."

"Would you give up this place for me?"

Catherine glanced away. "I suppose I have become a little bit attached. You're beautiful, you could convince me to do most things."

"Thank you so much." Isabella hugged her, feeling the other girl rigid in her arms.

"Are you a little bit scared of me?"

"Scared? No, no. I've known you since you arrived here. I've watched you grow into this confident young woman. By the time I realised how I felt, it seemed as if you were slipping away from me. It was as if Elizabeth read my mind, and invited me to draw you. I thought that drawing you would let me keep a little bit of you, forever. It ended up being more than that."

"How so?"

"I didn't know that I was going to end up drawing you like that. It made me feel closer to you and I knew that I was going to end up saying something."

"Well, I'm glad you did. You're a sweet girl."

"I know who you are, and the life that you are leading, so if you want to let me play a part in that, I would be so happy."

"Catherine, if I run again, please run with me."

"I will, Isabella," Catherine whispered, leaning over to Isabella, and clasping her hands in hers. "Don't marry anyone."

"I won't marry anyone, it isn't me."

They kissed. It was gentle and sweet, their lips barely grazing. Isabella felt the warmth of her lips and the wet of her drool.

"Sweet, sweet girl," Isabella whispered.

"That's you," Catherine replied.

Isabella kissed her forehead, "Share my bed tonight."

"I've been waiting for you to say that."

• • •

Isabella tried to push the idea of running out of her mind. She thought about shoving all her new beautiful clothes into a bag, and slipping down the stairs, as silent as she could. Opening the door, and glancing back up the stairs, knowing that it wouldn't be her home anymore. She didn't want to leave. She picked up her pillow, smelling the freshness of the bedsheets. There would be so many things to miss about the house and the people. Her master and Mistress, Garrett, and Catherine. At least she would be able to take Catherine, and her clothes, everything else would have to be left behind. And where would she go? She imagined wandering the roads and sleeping in hedges. Catherine would get miserable, and regret coming with her. Isabella shook her head, trying to get rid of her awful thoughts. There was no point in imagining disaster. She had to wait to see what would happen. If her father said yes to Garrett, she could stay at Mordancross House.

Isabella was on the bed, wrapped in a nightgown by the time Catherine came in. Isabella had thought about that first night that she had spent at the house, so she had run a bath for the two of them.

Catherine undressed out of her uniform, down to her chemise, and they stood in the bathroom, watching the long mirror steam up. As the water flowed in, Isabella added some oils, and bubbles formed. The water was too hot, so they had to wait. Catherine was facing the mirror, Isabella barely visible behind her, because of the steam on the glass. Isabella helped her slip out of her chemise. Her breasts were small and round, and the lines from the bones of her corset drew down along her back and her stomach. Her hair looked brown in the candlelight. Isabella unbuttoned Catherine's drawers, letting them fall around her ankles.

Isabella wanted to bury herself in Catherine's soft skin.

Isabella slipped into the water, only wincing slightly.

Catherine dipped one foot in. "Ouch."

Isabella looked up at her, and Catherine raised her leg, bent at the knee, allowing her to see between her legs. The smooth, darker skin of her inner thighs, the eruption of curls formed a V below her stomach. The heat brought out a pinkness in her skin. Catherine climbed into the bath.

They sat in the bath, knees touching, looking into each other's eyes.

"Have you ever done anything like this before?" Isabella asked.

"You were my first kiss." Catherine smiled.

Sweet girl, Isabella thought. *I hope I never hurt your feelings.*

"Turn around," Isabella whispered.

Catherine turned, and Isabella opened out her legs and let Catherine lean against her, resting her head on her chest. They listened to the crackle of the bubbles and the drip of the water from the tap. Isabella stroked Catherine's shoulders, feeling her sigh. She stroked her wet hair, down over her breast, feeling the hardening nipple. Isabella ground against Catherine's back, and she moved her hand down.

"Do you want me to?" Isabella asked.

"Yes, yes!"

She ran two fingers down over her clit, smiling to

herself, as she heard Catherine breathe in anticipation. She circled the clit, and Catherine opened her legs wider, knees touching the sides of the bath. Isabella felt Catherine's back arch against her, and Isabella pressed her lips to the other girl's neck, inhaling the sweetness of her skin. With her left hand, Isabella moved between Catherine's legs. The wetness of her arousal felt different to the water. Catherine's breathing was getting heavier as Isabella's fingers entered her.

"Oh, Isabella," Catherine whispered. "You have no idea how much I have wanted this."

Isabella smiled to herself. She was happy to be leading, and she wanted to make Catherine's first time as lovely as possible.

She pushed one finger inside, continuing to run her other fingers over her clit.

"How do you touch yourself?" Isabella asked. "Is it like this?"

"I've never put my fingers in myself before…"

"Do you trust me? Do you want me to?"

"Yes, I do, don't stop."

Catherine turned her head and kissed her, her breaths coming harder and heavier, her fingers clutching at Isabella's arms and hair.

"I was so jealous of her," Catherine breathed. "That she could have you whenever she wanted to. I'd see your bed empty and know that she was fucking you. I was jealous but thinking about it made me desire you more."

"Mmmm," Isabella sighed. "I'm sure you would have loved to watch, maybe draw her?"

"Oh yes," she replied breathlessly. "Draw her fucking you."

"Draw her, with her fingers deep in me," Isabella said, sliding her fingers in and out of Catherine. "And have you, reflected in the mirror, your pretty bright eyes watching as she ravages me."

"Oh yes, Miss Isabella, I want to see her all over you."

"And then I fuck you afterward? When you are all dripping wet from watching? So that you are all ready for me?"

Isabella felt Catherine tighten around her with arousal, her cheeks reddening.

"Cum for me, thinking about the Mistress, and me, and you." Isabella smiled, feeling the confidence radiating from herself.

"I will, I will," Catherine moaned, she pressed her back harder into Isabella.

Catherine was breathless, arching her back, her eyes closed and her mouth open, as she orgasmed. She lay in Isabella's arms in the cooling water.

"I can't believe that we did this." Catherine smiled.

"Well, I'm honored to have been your first."

They dried off together, sitting on Catherine's bed. Catherine opened the curtains wide. The rest of the house was in darkness, and there were no clouds in the sky.

"Do you know anything about the stars, Isabella?"

"I've never really thought about them."

"Well, if you look up above the big tree at the end of the lane, you'll see one flashing red, that's Betelgeuse."

"Stars can be red?"

"Of course. They form all kinds of beautiful patterns in the sky."

"I wonder how big they are. Are they huge like the sun, or could you hold them in the palm of your hand?"

"I don't know," Catherine admitted. "I read a book about stars, but I didn't understand most of it. I liked the pictures though."

"You'll have to find out more," Isabella said. "So, you can tell me all their names as I fall asleep."

Chapter 19

Catherine was dressing by the time Isabella woke up. Her narrow bed was still warm from her body.

"Lucky girl, getting to sleep in," Catherine said with a wry smile.

She bent down and placed a kiss on Isabella's bare shoulder.

"Don't sleep in too late." Catherine winked. "I don't want you to miss your breakfast."

"I won't," Isabella murmured back, her face still in the pillow.

"I know you wouldn't. You are seriously lucky that I am into lazy girls."

"Are you?"

"Of course. I'd get you up, I'd brush your hair and get you dressed, it would be my pleasure."

"And you would dress me up in whatever you wanted?"

"You know that I would. I would dress you like the sweet countryside girl that you are."

Isabella let out a short laugh. "Is that how you see me?"

"Yes, I see you in sweet floral dresses, sipping tea in a lovely garden."

"That is a lovely dream," Isabella whispered.

Catherine kissed her cheek. "It's not a crazy dream."

Isabella had fallen back to sleep, and by the time she woke up, Catherine was gone. She dressed into a cotton dress with a floral pattern, something simple compared to how she usually liked to dress. As soon as she got downstairs, a maid shyly told her that Garrett was looking for her. Rather than seeming too eager, she smiled and nodded. She would have breakfast before going to seek him out. She sat down at the long wooden bench and tried to force herself to eat. Her stomach was doing backflips. She managed to eat half a slice of dry toast. She could pretend all she wanted that she didn't want to know what Garrett had to tell her. She didn't know what she wanted him to say. The idea of marriage scared her, but if her father would let her forget all about the meek Phillip, she would be so thrilled. Phillip's pallid face made her stomach churn. She sipped at a cup of tea before giving in, accepting that she needed to go and see Garrett.

Outside, there was a drizzle, and the rain clung to her face. As she opened the stable door, she could hear Garrett singing to himself, mumbling the words to "I am the Monarch of the Sea". She listened and thought that he had a nicer voice than she would have imagined. He was sitting on the ground, polishing up a pair of the Mistress' boots. He stopped singing as soon as he saw her.

"Good morning, Garrett."

"It's good to see you, Isabella."

"I was told that you were looking for me?"

"Yes, I was, I wanted to tell you that your father replied to my letter."

That was what she had expected him to say, but the words still made her heart race.

"And what did he say?"

"Do you want me to read it to you?"

She nodded, dreaded thinking of him, sitting in his study, at the writing desk, putting pen to paper as he read over what Garrett had written. Garrett unfolded the letter from his back pocket, his face giving nothing away as he scanned the page.

"Dear master Garrett Lance, I was surprised to receive your letter, especially on the topic of my only daughter, Isabella."

She winced, even at the opening. Garrett was speaking in a deliberately formal tone, which usually would have made her laugh.

"I was interested to read of your desire to marry her, and the list you made of her positive traits did not seem like the girl that I raised. I will be honest with you, master Lance, Isabella's prospect for marriage has not been the best. She is a lazy girl, and she is not well-read or interesting. Her recent behavior has not helped, with her running away from home and pursuing a life of debauchery. Fortunately for young Isabella, a young solicitor in training, Phillip Dun, still has some space in his heart for her. A solicitor, as you can imagine, is a bit better than a stable boy."

Garrett glowered over the top of the letter as he read that line.

"So," he continued reading, "until I am lowered to the desperation of marrying my only child off to a stable boy, I will politely decline your offer. Isabella is my daughter and my property, and I will do with her what I see to be correct. I am sure you will understand that I will choose to disregard your advice. I will be calling to the house soon to bring Isabella home; she has been sorely missed. I wish you the best of luck in finding a wife more suited to your situation."

An uneasy silence hung between them, and Garrett crumpled the letter with one hand.

"Sorely missed?" Isabella exclaimed. "Perhaps they miss my cooking and cleaning."

She found herself shaking with rage. "I shouldn't be shocked that he writes about me like that. I'm sorry about what he said about you. There's no shame in doing honest work. He wouldn't know anything about that. He just wants people to listen to him, as he stands up as his podium."

"Don't worry about what he said about me, Isabella. I don't know what I was expecting, really. He was never going to say yes to me. You, however, have something to worry about."

"I know, his threat of coming to get me. That is the most pressing concern."

"What are you going to do?"

"I need to take my mind off it for the minute."

Isabella stroked Bracken's nose, as Garrett slipped off upstairs. She felt a tightness in her chest, and her anger had not yet disappeared. A life of debauchery? What would he know about that? She heard Garrett struggling back down the stairs a few moments later.

"I brought you a little something," he said, setting out a picnic blanket on the clean ground. "I wanted to show you that I'm not completely useless."

On the tartan blanket, he set out two tin mugs and some slightly crushed cream buns. He darted back up the wooden stairs and returned with a teapot. The tea was weak, but it didn't matter. She wiped the cream from the edge of his mouth, making him smile. She licked it from the edge of her finger.

"You're going to miss me, Isabella," he whispered.

"I will."

"When you are in the parlor of your solicitor's house, you will think of me and the life you had here."

"I'll never be in that parlor, Garrett, don't tease me!"

"I like a bit of teasing, anyway, you are the one leaving me, let me be angry with you."

He was looking into his teacup, so he didn't notice her getting up. His eyes opened wide as she straddled his hips. Her hair was tangled and frizzy from the rain, and it fell over her face.

"There's going to be no dull solicitor, there isn't going to be a stuffy parlor!" Isabella said.

"Are you sure, Isabella?" Garrett smiled, placing his hands on her hips. "If I try very hard, I can imagine you, oh I don't know? Rearranging doilies?"

"Doilies? I'll rearrange you!"

Garrett rolled over onto his side, pulling her down next

to him. "If you need help, you know that I would help you run, again."

"I appreciate that."

"I'm not asking anything from you. I don't want anything. I'd rather that I never saw you again than know that you were trapped with someone who doesn't suit you."

She had one leg over him, and the concerned look on his face suited him.

"There is something that I would like before I have to go anywhere," she said.

"And what is that?" His eyes were wide and honest, despite his attempts at teasing her.

"I want to fuck you."

His cheeks reddened, and he glanced downward. "I have wanted you for so long."

"I fantasised about you before I even knew your name, back in my bedroom in the parsonage."

She got back on top of him and kissed him, feeling his eagerness as his lips parted. He closed his eyes, managing to ignore the cold of the floor through the blanket. She pushed his hair off his face and traced down his cheekbones, down his slim neck, and feeling his pounding pulse through the skin. She felt his hardness through his ridiculously tight trousers. She reached down, pulling up her layers of skirts and petticoats, spreading them over him.

"Aren't you worried that someone will catch us?" he murmured.

"Not really." She smiled. "I'm far enough into my life of debauchery, but we can go upstairs if you like."

She was interested to see where he spent his nights.

The stairs were narrow, and her dress felt too big as she made her way up after him. The room was small, with a slanted ceiling.

"It's cosier than it looks, I promise," he said. "I hope that I don't bore you. I know that you are used to so much more."

"Don't be boring then." She winked.

He lay back on the bed, and with one hand, she unbuttoned her drawers, wriggling them down her legs and dropped them to the floor. She climbed on top of him.

"Yesterday, when Mistress Elizabeth was punishing us," she whispered. "I was hoping that I would be able to fuck you. Maybe you would have taken me over the saddle stand."

"Oh, Isabella, you have no idea how much I wanted that."

She held his wrist down with one hand as she unbuttoned his jodhpurs. She slipped her hand in, knowing that he wouldn't be wearing anything underneath. She felt the rough curls of his pubic hair, then the firm base of his cock. She let out a little gasp as she ran her fingers up its length. This encouraged a crooked smile from him. She drew it out from his trousers and glanced down, and she saw his thick, long cock, amongst all her layers of clothing. She leaned forward, her opening on the head of his cock. He let out a moan, biting his lip as she moved her hips, the soft head touching her clit, then down to the wetness between her legs. She held it there, the first inch of hard cock in her wet opening watching his expression. She knew that he wanted to grab her hips and pull her down, filling her up with his length. She had other ideas. They had been waiting so long, desiring each other; they could wait a few more minutes.

"Isabella, you'll kill me," he whispered.

She could hear the lust when he said her name, making her want to drool. The idea of his desire for her was such an erotic feeling. She loved knowing that he wanted her just as much as she wanted him. She remembered taking a bath, just before she had run away, and fantasising about him. He seemed to be living up to what she had thought. His breath quickened as she pressed down onto him, and a moan escaped her mouth, as the head of his cock pushed past her lips and into her. In a single movement, she was filled deep with his cock. They were still for a second, enjoying the feel of each other. Isabella felt the heat from his body, as she tightened around him. She watched the rise and fall of his chest as he watched her, tightening his fingers on the fabric of her dress.

With both of her feet on the bed, she lifted herself up, feeling his hardness move out of her, the movement of his penis in her, making her tremble. She was on top of him, the head of his cock was the only part inside her, until she pressed down onto him again, her buttocks and his hips meeting. His wide eyes betrayed his desire. She raised herself again, lingering on the slow draw out of his cock, feeling the perfect head as it traced along her insides.

"I've fantasised about you everywhere on this estate," Garrett whispered. "Tying me to a bed in one of those fancy bedrooms, and up here, of course. Now let me see you with nothing on."

He helped her undress, all nervousness gone. She sat up on the bed and watched him undress. He teased her, being slow with the buttons of his shirt. She was allowed to look this time, so she didn't mind. He unveiled his collarbones, his firm chest and his stomach, and she looked up at him. He had an almost smug grin on his pretty face. Taking off his tight trousers was less seductive. He had her pull his long boots off before he rolled his jodhpurs down his strong legs, leaving him stunning and naked. She pulled him back onto the bed, kissing him again. She froze, thinking she had heard a door open downstairs. She shushed Garrett. She was breathing heavily, and she had to steady herself. There was the sound of heels on the paved stone floor.

"Maybe if we are very quiet, whoever it is won't know we are here," Garrett whispered.

Isabella reached for her floral dress, hoping to hastily pull it back on. The bed creaked as she reached across it. She froze at the sound, wincing.

"Garrett?" the Mistress called. "I need your help with something." Isabella looked over at him, knowing that he wouldn't be able to ignore her. "I'm just up here," he called down.

The Mistress stepped onto the bottom stair. "What are you doing up there?"

Garrett threw Isabella a worried look before trying to pull his shirt back on. Isabella knew she wouldn't be able to get her dress on in time.

"I guess I should have known that you would be up here, Isabella." Elizabeth smiled.

"I am proud of you two for giving into your lusts. Don't let me interrupt."

"Oh," Garrett started, his hands concealing his erection. "It's all right, we were finished."

Isabella did not attempt to cover any parts of herself. She sat, cross-legged on the rumpled bedsheets, looking her Mistress in the eye.

"That's disappointing, Garrett." Elizabeth smiled. "Usually, Isabella is much more exhausted-looking when I am finished with her. Would you care to show me what you have between your legs?"

Despite his nervousness, he was still rock hard when he moved his hands away.

"It does not look like you are quite finished," Elizabeth said. "So, I think you should lie back against the headboard."

He did as she said, still wearing his half-buttoned shirt. The Mistress took Isabella by the jaw, opening her mouth by pushing fingers into the sides. She guided Isabella to Garrett's cock. The Mistress sat behind her on the bed, pushing her head down, and pulling her hips up. Isabella glanced up as she took his cock into her mouth, tasting herself on him. She saw his eyes widen.

Behind her, the Mistress wet her fingers in her mouth. She traced along Isabella's buttocks, leaving a trail. She found Isabella soaking wet. Her moans were stifled because her mouth was filled up, and Isabella shuddered as the two fingers were slammed into her, almost making her choke.

"Is she good, Garrett? Is she working hard enough?"

Isabella stole a glance-up at him as he replied, feeling him throb.

His voice was heavy and breathless. "She is, she is."

"Good," Elizabeth purred. "Such a talented girl, always so eager to please."

Isabella let herself be pulled back by her Mistress, who kissed her on the mouth, her face wet with spit. She lay Isabella back on the bed, her head on Garrett's flat pillows. The Mistress gripped the bed frame and sat on Isabella's face. Using her tongue and lips, Isabella navigated her, tasting the sweetness of her opening on the end of her tongue. The softness of her skin, hot and delicate.

Isabella thought that Garrett's hands should have been rougher. Instead, his touch was light and gentle, as he ran his hands from her knees, down toward her inner thighs, parting her legs. He entered her, just as she was closing her lips around Elizabeth's clit, her thighs wrapped tightly around her head. Elizabeth gripped a lock of Isabella's hair; the other hand was on the bed frame. Elizabeth rocked her hips forward and backward, the bed creaking under their weight. Garrett was inside her as deep as he could be, and Isabella felt his cock flex and throb inside her. His warm hands gripped her hips, as he pulled his cock out of her.

She couldn't think. All she knew was that she wanted to be used by both of them.

She was overwhelmed by the feeling of Elizabeth, grinding onto her, harder and harder. Isabella licked and sucked, placing her hands on Elizabeth's round hips, pressing her fingers in. She could hear her Mistress crying out in pleasure.

That's from me, Isabella thought. *I'm the one who gets to do this.*

As well as her Mistress, she could hear Garrett's moans of pleasure as he pressed back into her.

She couldn't believe that she was finally getting fucked by him. It wasn't quite how she had imagined, but she wouldn't have known to dream of something like that, those few months ago.

Garrett's hips were pressed against her, his firm buttocks barely trembled as he ploughed in and out of her, her wetness growing with each thrust. She knew that his view must be excellent, as he fucked her, seeing her squirming, naked body, as he pushed himself into her again and again. He couldn't see her expression, and her moans were muffled by the stunning woman on top of her. Isabella was buried under layers of skirts, intoxicated with the smell of Elizabeth's clothes and skin. Isabella moved one hand from her Mistress' hip, feeling the roundness of her buttock, and then down, feeling the space between her legs, so wet from arousal and spit. Two of her fingers slipped easily inside, and she felt her clench around her.

She withdrew, and then put three in, feeling her shift on her. Leaning back, grinding harder. She heard her Mistress calling her name, as she came on her face, feeling the grip around her fingers.

Isabella was gasping and writhing under Elizabeth, as Garrett continued to fuck her. Elizabeth dismounted, her skirts falling back around her. This revealed Isabella's red and gasping face to Garrett. He pushed his hair out of his face, and his eyes lingered on her. He gripped her hips harder, her arms were thrown back, and she looked up at him, a sly smile on her lips. Elizabeth admired herself in the slim mirror on the table, using it to glance behind her, at Garrett and Isabella.

Elizabeth put her hair behind her shoulders and smiled. A moment later she had her finger to Garrett's lips, stopping him. She lay him down beside Isabella, a tight fit on the narrow single bed. In one hand, she held two of the dark ribbons from her hair. She slipped the first ribbon around Isabella's wrists. Isabella looked up at her in confusion.

"This isn't too tight, is it?" Elizabeth asked.

Isabella shook her head. Garrett watched with uncertainty.

Next, Elizabeth sat on Garrett's lap, as she took his wrists in her slim hands. She bound his wrists close together.

"Is that all right?" she asked.

He nodded, not knowing what to say.

The apples of her pale cheeks reddened as she let out a small smile. Elizabeth felt Garrett's hardness against her. She placed his hands on his stomach, bound so he could not reach his hard cock.

"A bit of teasing is always fun, isn't it?" she asked, raising one eyebrow.

Garrett and Isabella glanced at each other, touching shoulder to shoulder, all the way down, Isabella could feel his lean, firm body pressed against her. His eyes glittered, and his mouth was open slightly. She was thrilled to finally be with him yet another experience that she would never forget.

As she gazed at him, she felt her Mistress part her legs. The tips of her fingers were warm and soft, opening Isabella's legs, exposing her. Isabella looked down at her Mistress, who lay between her legs. Elizabeth's ankles crossed over each other. She leaned up on her elbows, one hand on Isabella's inner thigh. She trailed her fingers along Isabella's soft skin, then confidently parted her lips, finding her hot, wet core. Elizabeth bit her lip as she slipped two slim fingers into her. Isabella felt Garrett's hot breath on her neck, as he watched as the Mistress fingered Isabella. He couldn't do anything about how he was feeling, with his wrists bound so tight. Her soft moans, as the Mistress put her mouth to work, made him harder than he ever thought was possible. Isabella arched her back as Elizabeth pushed herself into her. Garrett could hear the slick sounds of Elizabeth's fingers, drenched in her spit and Isabella's cum. He let out a groan of desire and desperation. He felt the throb and ache as Isabella tilted her head further back, her wrists bound, pushing her breasts together "Frustrated, Garrett?" Elizabeth asked, red curls falling around her shoulders, as she raised her head from the quaking Isabella.

Garrett nodded desperately.

"You don't mind waiting a moment, do you, Isabella?"

She nodded, but her eyes said otherwise.

It was Isabella's turn to be frustrated, as Elizabeth got on top of Garrett's calves. The dark heels of her shoes poked out from under her dress. She gripped his hands with one elegant hand. He watched her, breathlessly, as her hand slid down his length, gripping the base, and opening her full lips. Isabella would have been able to touch herself if she wasn't tied up. Instead, she watched Elizabeth's mouth on Garrett's cock, the pinkness of her tongue, quick as it darted in and out, teasing him.

"Oh God," Isabella whispered, squeezing her knees together.

She saw the Mistress' mouth curl up in a smile.

Isabella pushed her thighs together, trying to feel some friction, as Garrett cried out in ecstasy, thrusting into Elizabeth's mouth, as he orgasmed.

Elizabeth wiped her mouth on the back of her hand. She pressed her hot lips against Isabella's as she opened her mouth. The hot, salty liquid flowed into Isabella's mouth.

Elizabeth gripped her jaw as Isabella swallowed it. With one hand, Elizabeth was able to untie Garrett's hands, and Elizabeth beckoned to him. Within seconds, Isabella felt the sweetness of his mouth back on her clit.

"I am the best at it," Elizabeth whispered. "But I wanted to be able to look at you."

Garrett pushed his fingers inside, and as Isabella opened her mouth, her Mistress pressed her lips to hers. The tips of their tongues met, and Isabella lay, head tilted back, in a lazy, wet kiss with Elizabeth, while Garrett worked his fingers in, forcing hot breaths out of her.

"You will never forget me, Isabella," Elizabeth whispered, the tip of her tongue on Isabella's ear lobe.

"Never."

"And no one compares to me?"

"No one."

"Poor girl, I have ruined you." Elizabeth smiled.

Isabella looked at Elizabeth. Her eyes sparkled, as she held Isabella tight to her, her confident smile always leaving Isabella weak.

"I am sure he is not as good as me," Elizabeth whispered.

"No one could be," Isabella whispered back, although she could feel herself getting close.

She closed her eyes, feeling the tightness of the ribbon on her wrists. Garrett's tongue and sweet mouth, his fingers in her. Elizabeth took Isabella's lower lip in her mouth, the feel of the point of her tongue. The softness of Isabella's body against the firm bones of the Mistress' clothes. Isabella's frustration was released in an explosion, wrapping her legs around Garrett as she came. She lay breathless on Garrett's narrow bed. She felt Elizabeth's and Garrett's eyes on her face, the redness that had spread down her neck and onto her chest.

Elizabeth untied Isabella's wrists.

"You had better get dressed again, beautiful." Elizabeth sighed.

"Why?"

"I believe that you have a long day ahead."

Chapter 20

As her Mistress laced her back into her corset, Isabella asked what she was talking about. Garrett was buttoning his loose linen shirt back up. In the tiny mirror on the table, Isabella saw Elizabeth's expression change, her eyes narrowing and her mouth forming into a tight line.

"I was unfortunate to receive a letter from your father."

Isabella gasped and turned to face Elizabeth.

"He is not going to let you stay here, Isabella." Elizabeth sighed. "As much as I wish he would."

"What does that mean? What is he going to do?" Isabella asked, panic rising.

"He wrote that he is coming to get you. He is bringing a lawyer and a police officer, to take you home, away from me."

"What? When?"

"Today."

Isabella's knees almost gave up. "No! Can't you do something?"

"Legally, there is nothing that I can do."

"Don't say that!" Garrett interrupted.

"You are not letting me finish, Garrett," the Mistress said, raising an eyebrow. "There is something a bit less legal and a bit more dangerous that we can do, if you will trust me?"

"I'll try anything," Isabella said, pulling her dress on.

"I have asked Catherine to prepare your things for you, although I imagine that she may need some help. She has said she wants to go with you."

"I know, we spoke about it."

"Garrett is going to get a carriage ready, and he will take you to Dover."

"Dover?" Isabella asked.

"Yes," Elizabeth said. "You are to sail to France."

"If you would allow it, Mistress Elizabeth," Garrett said, "I would like to go with Isabella."

Elizabeth looked at him for a moment. "It will be a great loss to us, having all three of you leave, but I know that you will be good company for sweet Isabella."

Outside, there was the sound of a horse trotting up the driveway and the creak of cartwheels in need of oil. Isabella, Garrett, and Elizabeth froze where they were.

"You have to hurry, Isabella," Elizabeth said, hastily fastening the hooks and eyes on the back of Isabella's dress.

Isabella could not stop herself from shaking as she hurried across the courtyard. The cart was pulling in between the pillars as Isabella pushed the door open. She caught a glimpse of the occupants of the cart. Her father sat, holding the reins of the horse. Beside him sat a heavily built police constable and Isabella's skinny and wan fiancé. She felt a lurch in her chest as she pulled the door closed behind her. As she ran up the front stairs, there was a pounding at the door. She met the master of the house on the landing.

"What is wrong, Miss Isabella?"

"Oh, my father is here to get me!"

"Don't worry, I will keep him distracted. Go and get your belongings." He kissed her on the cheek.

"Thank you."

Catherine was folding Isabella's beautiful dresses into a suitcase. She had her own sitting on the floor ready.

"They are here, Catherine!" Isabella cried.

"Oh, shit," Catherine swore, a panicked expression on her face.

"Elizabeth is asking Garrett to get a carriage ready."

"It's going to be okay, Isabella," Catherine said. "It's all going to be fine."

"Of course, I know," Isabella said, shaking her head. She took a dress from the bed and hastily shoved it into the case.

The girls looked at each other as Isabella fastened the clasps. They grabbed a case each.

Isabella glanced around the corner at the top of the grand, sweeping stairs. At the bottom of the staircase, stood her father, a policeman, and her grim fiancé. Isabella gripped the wall. The master spoke to them in a calm tone.

"I am not sure where Isabella is at the moment," the master said. "She must be hard at work somewhere."

"I demand to see her!" her father said.

"I am sorry, she will be here as soon as anyone can locate her."

"Legally," the fiancé said, "you cannot conceal her from us. I cannot stand the idea of my wife to be slaving away in this house, especially with the reputation it has. She should be at home."

"You are a very lucky young man," the master said with a laugh. "Isabella is wonderful. I am sure that she will make you very happy."

"We shall see, having a wife is important for appearances. We are looking forward to having her home as soon as possible."

"Isabella," Catherine whispered, "I know that you want to listen, but we need to get away from here."

"Okay, the back stairs."

The handle of the case clunked, and Phillip looked up, narrowing his small eyes.

"There is someone there."

He slipped around the master, who had put out an arm to stop him.

"Is that the man who wants to marry you?" Catherine asked, pulling at her arm.

"My fiancé," Isabella said, rolling her eyes.

"We can't let him see you!"

"I know there's someone up there!" Phillip yelled, a tremble in his voice. "Isabella, is that you?"

Isabella almost pushed Catherine to the floor in panic. Catherine grabbed her hand and pulled her along the corridor.

"Where are we going?" Isabella asked.

"We can't use the front staircase. We will get caught."

"I'd read in a book that sometimes staircases and corridors would be concealed in the walls? Maybe it's true?"

"Well, that is all we have to go on."

They reached the end of the corridor, and they started to feel around on the walls. The wooden panels were ornate, with curls of roses and leaves covering it.

"Isabella!" Phillip called from behind. "There you are, at last. Everyone at home has been so worried about you."

Isabella turned to see him hurry up the hallway, top hat in hand. She let go of the handle of the suitcase in surprise.

"You are so pretty. I am excited to see you learning to behave. I am hoping that your parents teach you some discipline before they hand you over to me." Phillip grabbed her wrist. "Come on, Isabella, it is time to go home, and when everyone in the village has just about forgotten about your little transgressions, then we can get married."

"Let go of me! What has happened to you? You don't even know me!"

"I was trying to make a good impression the first time I met you. Now I know what is rightfully mine."

Isabella's other arm was gripped by Catherine, who had discovered a door handle built into the wooden panelling. She pulled the door open slightly and tossed a suitcase in.

"We can't stay, Isabella," Catherine said, gripping Isabella's arm with both hands.

Isabella felt Phillip's fingers dig into her, not letting her go. The fabric in her sleeve strained, ripping at the shoulder. Phillip lost his grip, and Catherine pulled her through the door. Catherine shut the door so quickly that she almost caught Phillip's fingers. He cried out in anger and pounded at the door. Isabella looked up at Catherine's panicked face, as she strained, holding onto the door handle.

"I didn't get the other suitcase!" Isabella cried.

"Is that all you can think about?" Catherine asked. "Help me out here."

"Of course, what's wrong with me?"

Isabella put her hands over Catherine's, feeling Phillip pulling against them on the other side of the door.

"He has to give up, doesn't he?" Catherine whispered.

"He will, he must."

"I won't give up," Catherine said, leaning down to kiss her.

The corridor was dark and dusty, and a cobweb tickled Isabella's nose. Catherine was on the top stair, and Isabella was on the one below her, pressed together. It almost felt like they were playing about together, avoiding work.

Through the door, they could hear Phillip speaking to someone, and the pulling stopped.

"She is through here."

"We have to go," Catherine said.

As soon as they let go, the door swung open, letting in the bright light of the landing.

"Run, Isabella!" Catherine hissed.

Phillip glanced around to see Isabella, followed by Catherine, suitcase in hand.

Isabella did not know where the stairs would lead them. It curved around, and her hair was filled with dust and webs. They reached a dead-end, and Catherine stumbled into the back of Isabella. Isabella ran her hands over the wall as her heart pounded in her ears. Footfalls thudded on the old wooden steps behind them. Catherine let out a yelp of excitement; she had found the door handle. They clattered out into the downstairs servants' corridor, near the kitchen. Isabella slammed the door behind them, hoping it would take Phillip a few minutes to find the handle.

Catherine took Isabella's hand in hers, their heels clicking on the tiled floor, as they made their way to the back door. In the courtyard, Garrett sat at the front of the grand carriage, reins in hand.

"Where have you been?" Garrett yelled. "They are here, they are in the house!"

"I know!" Isabella shouted back. "Hopefully, we have outrun them!"

Garrett shifted to the right of the bench on the front of the carriage. Isabella put one foot on the step. It was so thin that it trembled under her weight. She took the suitcase from Catherine and passed it up to Garrett, who opened the window into the carriage and tossed it in. Catherine was struggling to get up; the height of the carriage step was tough for a short girl. Isabella grabbed both of her hands.

"You don't have time, Isabella," Catherine cried.

"Shush!" Isabella hissed back. "We are running together, now come on."

Isabella managed to pull her up, falling back into Garrett. In that second, Phillip appeared at the back door, followed by Isabella's father.

"Garrett! They are going to get us!" Isabella said, panicking. "You need to get us out of here."

Garrett flicked the reins and smiled at her; the dark

horse broke into a trot. "I wouldn't worry too much; I blocked their cart in with a couple of barrels."

Isabella glanced over her shoulder to see her father and fiancé gesturing angrily, as the policeman tried to roll the barrels out of the way.

"That doesn't mean that we can take our time," Catherine said, folding her arms. "I am sure that they will be on our trail as soon as they can be."

"You're right," Garrett replied. "They will be keeping an eye out for carriages with the Mistress' crest."

As they rounded the side of the house, Isabella saw her former master and Mistress standing on the doorstep. Elizabeth smiled and blew her a kiss. Isabella watched them, as the horse brought the carriage past the front of the house and towards the gates.

"Are you going to miss her?" Catherine asked, looking up into Isabella's eyes.

"Of course," Isabella said. She slipped one arm around Catherine and the other around Garrett, who was focused on the road. "But I have the pair of you, and I think that the goodbye to my lovely Mistress doesn't mean forever."